A Problem of Ghosts

Miranda Mayer
www.mirandamayer.com

Content Editing:
Two Girls Friday
www.twogirlsfriday.com

Cover Art by:
Mt. Hood Creations

Photography:
Orange Kraftwerks by
Sepp Bernhard
www.facebook.com/orange.kraftwerks

Models:
Lily Parker
Ryan Michael Pierson

Stylist:
Morgan Shanafelt
morganshanafelt.carbonmade.com

Costumes:
Lady's Costume
Mt. Hood Creations
Gentleman's Costume
Morgan Shanafelt

Photo Shoot Location:
Portland's White House
www.portlandswhitehouse.com

A Problem of Ghosts

A fantasy by

Miranda Mayer

BOOKS

Oregon

Dedications

To my many friends and partners in geekery. My world
is so much the better for knowing all of you.
Geek on.

Table of Contents:

BOOK 1
THE PROBLEM OF GHOSTS

Fallswell Hall had a ghost problem. It was so severe a ghost problem in fact, that the house was left in a state of near abandonment for two and twenty years until it was at last purchased by the widow Ammette. Until then, the care of the place was left to a senile caretaker by the name of Ekkin who was mostly deaf and occasionally delusional. It was likely his mental state that made it possible for him to remain at Fallswell all those years.

It wasn't that the widow was unaware of the ghost problem upon purchase, she was perfectly sensible to the various presences that resided in the old building. Widow Ammette was a keen seer of the dead. She always had been. It was merely that she could not be bothered by ghostly mischief. The estate was large and lovely with sweeping views of the mountains. The addition of some troublesome ghosts was not enough to deter her.

Although people could either see or hear ghosts and spirits by varying degrees; most did not possess widow Ammette's fortitude. Fallswell's ghosts were not difficult to see or hear by any measure. The strength of their haunting was beyond the pale, and because of that, they were quite bold and flagrant—and would test the resilience of the most unflappable souls.

In general, ghosts were not usually found in such vast numbers as could be found at Fallswell. In other parts of the world, one would be astonished to run into one or two here and there. Perhaps one could witness a few in a particularly potent area. The great isle of Mahalav was, however, infamous for its hotspots. Fallswell Hall happened to sit in an area where the *shadethers* were appallingly strong. The speculation was that the original builder had not been exceedingly sensitive to these things when he drew up his plans for the home, and began construction. He neglected to bring an etherman to prepare a survey of the shadether emissions of this estate—something any sensible builder ought to do. As a result of this gross oversight, after but a few generations of the resident family, the place was chockablock with disgruntled spirits.

The family grew weary of the moaning ranks of deceased relatives, servants and friends; so they packed up and left the stately hall for the agent to sell. It was a job that was handed down from father to son, for it took two decades to find someone willing to live with a horde of restless ghosts.

The widow was not impervious to fear. The critical aspect which made her compatible to this unusual house was that while the widow was sympathetic to the plight of her resident specters, she wasn't disposed to humor their persistent demands for attention. As an experienced and reputedly strict mother and grandmother, she was well versed in establishing respectful interactions; therefore, it took only a week or so of her living in the austere old edifice for the mischievous spirits to settle down into an acceptable routine where everyone, including the restive spirits, was content.

The routine sometimes fell into chaos when visitors came, for the presence of new people would disrupt the spiritual calm. That was why the widow did not invite guests into her home very often. She bought the home for the purpose of seeking peace and quiet, and managed to get the ghosts in her new home to conform to this desirable state.

The arrival of Miss Dae Evlan and her little sister Renna was one of those instances when the specters of Fallswell would have an ideal audience for their mischief, and for a while, the delicate balance was upset. Additionally, the girls were not to spend only a short time at Fallswell Hall, they would be staying indefinitely. The Evlan girls were the grand-nieces of the Widow Ammette.

They had never met their great aunt, as they had lived overseas at Garvash until recently, when both their mother and father were taken into custody for unspecified crimes against the crown. The family's possessions were confiscated, their grant rescinded, the title stripped and the children were given a choice of finding employment under their peers, or identifying a relative or guardian willing to take responsibility for them. Letters were hastily dispatched to various family members and it was settled that they would go to their Great Aunt Ammette Reyna for the time being. There was a lingering hope amongst the family that the lank-haired, bony-faced attorney that represented the Evlans' interests could adequately prove to the crown that the charges were erroneous and that this state would only be temporary. It was hoped, but in truth, it was not generally believed.

As to be expected, Dae and Renna were confused and distraught by the whole matter. Dae, a sensible, frank, and bright girl of nineteen acted as a governess of sorts to her fifteen year old sister. The attorney had endeavored to find them a suitable home, and had applied to many members of the extended family. The response was not enthusiastic, for nobody wished to be connected to the parents any longer—even if it meant spurning their innocent young girls. Aunt Ammette was suggested as a possible guardian by an uncle of the girls, and the attorney sent a query. Her reply to him was brief. "Of course they can come here. Send them to Fallswell. Notify me of their itinerary and I will have my coach at Ovonoth waiting for them when they arrive." Aunt Ammette took more time and care in her communication to the girls, which they received shortly before they were packed up and sent to sail to the isle of Mahalav where she lived.

The letter from Great Aunt was kind, and welcoming. She wrote the expected regrets for their troubling situation in the first paragraph; and another paragraph about her recollections of their parents. She scribed a small missive about the home to which they would be traveling. She had, however, been insufficient in giving warning to the girls about the spectral problem at their new home.

She had only made mention of "a minor haunting that may cause you a little initial disturbance." She went on to say, "nonetheless ghosts are everywhere, so it's nothing new. You and your sister must not concern yourselves with trifles, for the first and most pressing matter will be the task of finding a proper abigail, which in this part of the country are most difficult to find. Staffing the house continues to be a challenge three years on. I cannot see there are other sources of well-paid employment in the area to cause this deficit. It is a subject of continual frustration for me. But fret not girls, we will muddle through. We will muddle through."

Had Dae not been so overcome with concern for her present situation and that of her sister, she might have seen the forewarning in Aunt Ammette's complaints about her staffing problem. But she did not. She could only be overcome with relief that someone in their family was happy to have them—and that she would not have to suffer the humiliation of being employed by people who were her peers. This notion terrified her.

The girls arrived at Fallswell Hall mid-afternoon on an early winter day, just before a snow storm. After having spent the night in a shabby little inn and another six days in a rattletrap of a post coach and a succession of other, shabbier inns—preceded by a stomach-roiling ocean crossing on a creaky, leaky excuse for a passenger vessel that took eleven miserable days—the girls were quite disposed to be finished with all this traveling nonsense.

They were collected that morning at the cusp of dawn by their Aunt's fine coach. Its proper suspension, attentive livery and lively team softened the pains and discomfort brought on by the previous days of being shaken and tossed about. The team had been sent the previous day to ensure that the girls would have a comfortable conveyance for the final leg of their journey, and that they would be off at their earliest convenience. The coachman had even lined the seat bins with heated bricks so the cold would not be quite so biting.

"How thoughtful of our great Aunt," Renna exclaimed, settling into her seat after being handed in by the footman. "I have wondered if she is a reasonable woman. I think, after this morning, I am quite convinced that she is." Renna then looked around the inside of the plush coach with an approving smile. Dae arranged her book and her knitting basket beside her on the seat and then reached up to untie the net and lace veil that draped over her bonnet, knotted loosely under her delicate chin. She pulled it off, and folded it carefully before lifting the bonnet off of her lustrous sandy hair and setting it carefully by the other window. She reached for one of the wool throws and wrapped her legs in it.

"Being she is the only relative willing to take us in, after the disgrace mother and father have brought upon our family, I've concluded quite the opposite. No reasonable person would welcome such shame across their threshold. Therefore she must be most *un*reasonable, and for that I am *most* grateful," the elder sister replied. She watched Renna remove her gaudy hat and organize the projects she carried with her every day but hadn't touched. She too wrapped herself up. When her sister was done fidgeting about, Dae fluidly reached her arm across the divide, holding out her book. Renna took it with a scowl, and leafed through the pages.

The coachman and dapper footman finished loading the two humble trunks containing the girls' sparse belongings; they climbed up onto the bench together, and with little commotion, the handsome dapple greys cast the coach forward to Fallswell Hall. Renna's sweet voice accompanied the equipage all along the way, as she read to her sister. Dae's hands worked the needles. The coach kept a good deal of the cold at bay. Their legs and shoulders swathed in blankets and shawls, they found their journey quite tolerable. The sisters paused only in their reading and knitting to drink and eat from the modest hamper provided by the last inn, and to get out while the coach made a rest stop at a tavern by the river. The girls stretched their legs while the horses were refreshed.

By the time they reached the hall, they were ready for the forsaken journey to be over. The lingering warmth from the bricks had faded, and the blankets were just beginning to be insufficient against the deepening cold. Hoarse, Renna dreamt of a soft bed, a hot toddy and a warm fire. Fingers sore, Dae wanted nothing more than quiet and a new book to read. Instead, they were greeted at the steps by a solemn-faced Great Aunt, and a parade of frantic ghosts. One glance at the maelstrom of spirits twisting out of every door and window, and Dae emitted a most indelicate groan. "Oh, bloody hell," she muttered.

Both girls were prevented from immediately introducing themselves to their generous relative because of the veritable horde of spirits that immediately enfolded them. "Don't let the ghosts be a bother to you my dears, come inside. They will settle down in time. They become excited at new visitors," Aunt Ammette blurted, waving her hand dismissively and turning up the stairs to the entranceway. She spoke as if the whirling cloud of shrieking specters were naught but a small pack of dainty lap dogs jumping up on their legs. Dae could scarce see her little sister so flocked she was by seemingly angry ghosts.

Renna was growing increasingly frightened, and the spirits delighted in it, flying in a vortex around her until she looked to be invested in a tornado. "Aunt!" Dae cried. The elderly lady turned and with a sigh of great inconvenience, stamped in an unseemly fashion down the steps again and shooed the flitting forms away as if chasing off a murmuration of starlings. She then proceeded back up the steps and into the house, talking all the while.

"I found a girl, so you won't be completely without assistance. She is sadly a dim little creature who says little, but we can count that as a blessing for nobody cares for a chattering abigail. You both must be beyond fatigued. This chill will work to your advantage, for with the inevitable snow you will have plenty of time to rest and recuperate from your travels. I am quite certain your family and your attorney will appreciate an assurance of your safe arrival as well. You will have all the time you need to catch up on your correspondence..." her voice faded as she disappeared inside the house.

Renna and Dae clutched their baskets and scurried after her, shooing at the lingering ghosts, and slipping into the open doorway just before the footmen went through with their trunks. Aunt Ammette was already entering a doorway to the right, still chattering on. Dae gave her sister a glance of trepidation, and proceeded after her, with Renna at her heels.

"...Mivenos is not at all as cross as he looks, so don't hesitate to engage him and ask for whatever you need. Do take off your redingotes my dears, and those hats, goodness me, how the hats have gotten flamboyant these days, I dare say. Put them there, and your gloves as well, Mivenos or Mrs. Baque will see to them when they get to it. Without a scullery maid and the continued shortage of chamber maids, their labors are stretched very thin, you surely understand."

All the while that Aunt Ammette spoke, a large inky blot of a ghost hovered over her head like some perverse hat or coif. Tendrils of the ghost's body snaked down and made as if to caress her sharp cheeks and her rather tousled looking hair. She took no notice of the spirit. She merely crossed to the girls, who stood frozen, and began to help them to remove their outer-wear.

"Mousy little things," she muttered, pressing aside a few curls of Renna's dark brown hair. She lifted her chin and smiled at Renna's confused face. "Do not be sad my dear, nor you, my dear Dae. You are home now. Whether or not your parents' troubles are resolved, I am here for you. Come, take off that hat." She removed Dae's hat and then smiled at them both.

Aunt Ammette was a woman of sixty seven years. Her hair, once a similar dark chocolate brown to her great niece, was now silvery white, arranged in a slightly old-fashioned mass on the top of her head. Some bits were tidily curled, others looked frizzy and unkempt. Her face, wizened and kind, had lines indicating a lifetime of sweet expressions. Her eyes were a startling blue, and still bright and lively. Her nose, although rather large and aquiline, had nobility to it. She was a small thing, but she carried herself with grace. Her gown was a fashionable, beautiful draping of emerald silk. The elaborate and unmistakably rich jewelry adorning her neck and wrists, like her hair, were reminiscent of another time.

She in turn studied her new wards. The girls' eyes were locked on the ghostly headdress, but Ammette made no indication of awareness of her undulating companion. "I ordered tea the moment I saw the coach pass down the lane towards the park. So do sit my dears. Warm yourselves up." Somewhere in the depths of the house, there was a horrendous, bone chilling scream. It continued unabated and grew louder and louder as if it was approaching. Then suddenly a figure emerged from the wall near the hearth; a misty shape of a woman with a horrifying face with only gaping black holes for eyes and a mouth. It floated through the room making its deafening shriek before crossing through the outer wall to the front of the house and spooking the coach horses and the stable boy holding their bridles. Aunt Ammette stood with her hand gesturing to the sofa before the fire with a soft smile on her face. She then relented and sighed.

"Don't pay any heed to their antics dear girls, or they will never stop with the theatrics. Just sit and we will soon have tea." They sat, mouths agape. Even Renna, who never stopped talking, had nothing to say.

"Ortner, do keep your tentacles out of my face, I beg you," Ammette muttered, waving her hand in front of her face. "I do hope the excitement of your arrival will pass soon. They are all so intolerable right now. Ortner is especially clingy." At that moment Dae, who was known for being sensible and poised, burst into riotous laughter. The trauma of their ordeal, and the absurdity of their arrival, proved more than she could bear, and her response was to laugh merrily at it all. Renna gaped at her sister in puzzlement. Aunt Ammette merely joined her in her mirth. It was all they could do in the situation. They laughed, and then had tea as the housekeeper finally appeared carrying a tray and a tea towel that she was using to flick the curious spirits away.

The situation with the Fallswell ghosts provided various surprising benefits for the Evlan girls. For, contrary to typical ladies of their young blossoming age, the Evlan girls did not care for the niceties of society, nor were they drawn to the things other young women might find delightful. Balls and assemblies; merry parties, shopping, picnics, outings and teas; none of these things appealed greatly to either of them. This had been a matter of great frustration to their parents, who both hoped to see them elevated by good society and glowing marriage prospects. Both girls preferred solitude. They liked to read and knit, to make lace and draw. Dae liked to wander over the landscape and find wild things. Renna enjoyed exploring as well, and was a skilled climber of trees. They did not care for fashion or gossip.

Fallswell, being the only great house for many miles would have, if the circumstances were different, been a social hub for the uppity ups of the surrounding villages. However, because of its frightful state of haunting, hosting anyone of consequence was out of the question. No balls would be held in the stunning hall of the elegant manse, and no society peers would cast their shadow near the house that was literally seething with restless dead. The distance and the weather were also excuse enough for the girls to remain comfortably separated from the society scene. The irritation of the haunting was but a mote of an inconvenience for the girls, in light of all the burdensome things it helped them avoid.

The Evlans soon became accustomed to the spectral madness of this house, and learned to ignore screaming Imelda, and to smirk knowingly whenever Ortner materialized possessively over Ammette's head, and to quietly forbear the little annoyances created by the twins, who liked to scatter the girls' small things about their rooms. They came to know the individual ghosts as the winter days waxed. Some had names, others had stories. Almost all of the ghosts vied for the attention of the youthful residents. Some remained distant and brooding, and as the girls settled in, the desire to know about them all increased. It was a strange family of sorts. With all the time they did not waste socializing with their peers, they could freely dedicate their efforts to further understanding Fallswell and its many, many residents.

In the third week of their new residence, Dae was occupying herself by reorganizing the disaster that was Ammette's personal library. Although she had lived at Fallswell for three full years, she had yet to unpack or properly sort through a variety of crates and trunks, and her collection of books had been thrown haphazardly on the shelves of the graceful library without the slightest consideration for content or subject. Great Aunt had given Dae leave to sort it all out as Ammette had no inclination to do so, and her meager staff had not the knowledge or means. So she set to work as soon as a suitable fire was blazing in the hearth, and it was warm enough to work.

Kee had brought Dae a nice tray of refreshments to carry her through a few hours. So she poured herself a cup of piping hot tea, put the pot on the iron swivel by the fire to keep it hot, and tackled the first shelf. She rolled up the long sleeves of her burgundy wool day gown, and began sorting titles by categories. As she worked, a small timid ghost that Renna called Pipsqueak boiled up through the cabinet top, and began to roll around in the book stacks she was making.

There were various forms taken by ghosts. Some, like Ortner and Pipsqueak were the kind the girls called blots. They were in shape nothing more than inky, undulating balls of black mist, with occasional appendages that sometimes peeled off. There were the Imelda ghosts that seemed to take a form that is designed to frighten. The general shape of a body, perhaps with an indication of a frock or gown billowing after them; hair streaming and twisting like tentacles, hollowed eyes and mouth, sometimes even a skeletal head and bony hands with curls of smoke colored mist unfurling from their forms. Because of Imelda, Renna called these kind shriekers. They were loud and particularly annoying as they constantly presented a problem for the estate's animals, who never seemed to get used to them. Horses were unnerved; cows put off their milk, chickens off their eggs. Ammette was at present commissioning a new stable and barn to be built at the edge of the park where the etherman assured her there would be less activity of the supernatural kind.

The third kind, and the rarest, were the ghosts that resembled ordinary people. No skull faces, no shrieking passes, the quiet ones as Renna called them, would appear like a glow, faces clear, limbs sometimes, clothing reasonably recognizable. They would linger briefly looking sorrowful, and then fade. Ammette claimed that the blots would sometimes become quiet ones, if they were so inclined, and she said Ortner was sometimes disposed to transform into a kindly looking elderly gentleman with a large gin-blossom covered nose.

There were at least twenty blots out of the impossible number that they could recognize by routine and behavior. There were four shriekers, Imelda being the worst of the four, and seven to nine quiet specters, depending on whether one was actually posing as another. Dae knew Pip because of the way she tended to come out of walls and furniture as if she was water boiling up from a kettle and spilling herself into the room. She seemed to take interest in the task with which Dae was at present employing herself. While Pip flitted around the books, Dae quietly worked.

To her annoyance, Pip began to make mischief. Only the blots were strong enough to cause actual physical effects in the living world. Pip wasn't one that partook in these kinds of acts. The twins were at it all the time. Dae imagined they were ghosts of two mischievous young boys, for the spirit in which they acted felt like that is what they were. Pip was a timid little ghost. She followed Dae about occasionally. She would boil up onto the counter of her vanity while Dae did her hair, or seep like oil through the canopy of the bed and then sink into the mattress when she was lying in.

Pip toppled some books and flipped others open. With an annoyed sigh, Dae got up to tidy the mess and shoo the little ghostlet away. As she approached, the inky little blot fell over a book and wildly fanned its pages. The movement stopped abruptly on a particular page. A tendril of an arm formed from her smoky shape, and slithered out towards a lithograph of a young man holding a lady's hand. Dae's brow rose in puzzlement as she peered at the image. She took it in, and then looked at Pip's roiling shape.

"Do you like this book?" she asked. She closed the cover and studied the spine. "An Engagement for Evalee," she read, nonplused. "If it pleases you, Pip, I can read it to you, if that is what you wish. If you leave this table alone, I will gladly re…" The little ghost lashed out again and threw open another book and another. It pointed to one page, then the next. Dae pulled the first book over and peered at what the curl of mist indicated. It slid along three words embedded in a paragraph; "he wants to…" Dae read. Snap, the other book fell before her and the inky arm pointed to "hurt." Dae was surprised. "Who is he and whom does he wish to harm?" The misty arm snaked out and rested a hair above Dae's arm.

"Someone wishes to harm me?" The ghost roiled momentarily in what must have been frustration, and then threw open the Engagement for Evalee, to the same page as before, pointing to the gentleman. Dae arched her brow and pursed her lips. "What gentleman, Pip?" The ghost merely hovered for a moment and unexpectedly disappeared in a flit.

Puzzled, slightly alarmed, but undeterred, Dae refreshed her tea and returned to her task. Her mind was distracted by Pip's assertion. She wondered if perhaps Ammette might know what this was about. She resolved on asking at nuncheon, and set the matter aside for the time being.

"We have a letter," Renna exclaimed as her sister joined them at the table for lunch. Renna looked positively lovely in her grey linen with the sky blue tambour work on it. Her green eyes were bright with glee as she waved the letter at Dae. "It's from Mr. Howkes." Dae's initial pleasure faded at once. She did not want news from him. It simply could not be good, of that she was certain.

She sat while Renna, now at liberty to open the letter, did so. While Dae poured herself a goblet of cider and cut a slice off the cold ham, Renna proceeded to read the communication.

Esteemed Misses Evlan

I am corresponding with you as there is a development in the trial of your parents that requires that the representative of the throne interview the both of you. I have agreed to this as long as I am present during this interchange, and have agreed to accompany the representative to your current residence. We will be arriving on the fifth day of Hoguemoon, contingent of course on the steadiness of the sea. Please expect us to arrive at Fallswell sometime on that day in the late afternoon, as the post is scheduled. Please notify your guardian, as I understand there are no inns within reasonable distance, so we will have to impose upon her hospitality for the duration. I look forward to seeing the both of you healthy, and comfortably established. I will be able to report this good news to both your mother and father, who both miss you terribly.

I will see you soon, etc., etc. Figson Howkes, Atty at Law

"I fail to see what they stand to gain coming all the way out here to interview us. We don't even know the nature of the crime our parents are accused of; what use would it be to speak to us?" Dae snapped.

"Perhaps it is a matter of character witness. To paint a full picture of the kind of parents they were," Ammette opined. Renna, whose disappointment in the content of the letter had her holding back tears, merely looked on with glossy eyes.

"Well it's just stupid." Dae served herself a few spears of pickled asparagus and some soft cheese and bread, and she ate brusquely, her interchange with Pip duly forgotten. "What prosecuting attorney wants to paint a positive image of the accused?"

"Dae, don't be rude," Renna snapped. "Aunt was only offering a suggestion." Dae stopped mid chew and dropped her chin.

"Oh goodness, Aunt Ammette, I was not accusing you of anything. I apologize. I was just speaking my frustration. They have ignored us from the start, the attorney scrambling to send us away the very morning the militias came for them. Why we are suddenly of interest is just beyond me."

"Well we are soon to find out. They are arriving in four days," their guardian said with a decidedly resigned tone of voice. She was at present free of her frequent spectral companion, and was enjoying a cup of tea. The shaft of mid-day light streaming into the small, private dining room made her look younger, and cast golden hues on her silver side curls, and brightened the lacy cap adorning her head.

"We can rejoice in one thing, they do not know about Fallswell's ghost problem. We can expect that because of it the visit will be brief." Renna chuckled. Dae smiled too. As if on cue, Imelda started yowling somewhere upstairs. She startled someone, because the sound of a brief shout and smashing dishes followed. This was a daily occurrence. Ammette spent a fair sum on replacement ceramics.

Dae and Renna spent the following afternoon shopping for a couple of ladies' mounts. Ammette was an enthusiastic rider, and she felt for both of the girls being shipped off and forced to leave their beloved hacks behind to be sold. She wanted for the girls to ride with her, and arranged for the only horse trader in the county to bring some of his finer beasts to the stocks at Bembly for the girls to try. Bembly was a small village about eight miles from

Fallswell, and it too was purportedly a place of strong shadethers, so there were few residences, no inns, and only a shabby tavern which was not much more than an annex to an old goat barn with a few tables, benches, what was once a mash oven that served as a hearth, and a stack of beer barrels all tapped and ready to pour. As sparse as it was, it was reportedly always crammed with farmers at the end of each day.

The stock yards were scant and overgrown, the summer grasses flattened by frost, which gave the visiting herd something to occupy them while one horse was tacked up. The trader had only a mouse chewed sidesaddle, and a bridle made of sewn canvass. One of the girls at a time was thrown up onto the horns of the shabby saddle to ride the horse down the single lane and back. Although it was frigid outside, the girls had shed their redingotes as the brisk exercise of riding warmed them up.

"It's hard to really tell if I like a horse when the saddle is ill fitting. This one's withers are so high the saddle sits uphill." Renna grumbled, dropping down from a neat little bay. The chocolate coat was luminous and healthy, velvety in its winter fullness. Her raven tail and mane shone. The little mare had bright eyes and a nice conformation. Dae let the merchant throw her up. Renna was right, the saddle was a bad fit, but how the horse responded to her was more important. A new saddle was easily procured. Bad training, or physical flaws, those were more expensive problems. Dae found this mare was fluid and responsive, and even sitting uphill, the gaits were tolerable as she put her through the paces up and then down the lane. She cantered up to them, and with but a small indication, the horse halted square.

"I do like this one," she told the trader through a cloud of misty breath. "This one is the one I want." After six horses, this was the only one that resonated with Dae's subdued hand and light leg. She did not like to ride with a cane and wanted a horse that could understand her cues without one. This mare was it. She did not want to try any more horses. The merchant nodded silently and led the mare to tie her at the bar so Renna could try another. After a lazy chestnut, and a spooky black pony, Renna was put on a showy dapple gray gelding. His body was thick and round, his legs fine and delicate. Dae thought he suited Renna at once. Her radiant smile as she cantered him twice up the lane was all the confirmation Dae needed. Renna lingered on his back and patted his neck; whorls of steam rose up from his chest. "He is a handsome fellow," Dae declared.

"I think I like him more than West," she said with a guilty smirk. "Is that awful of me?"

"You've had West since you were eight. He was too small for you. You eventually outgrow your pony. It's only natural that you would like a higher quality animal sooner or later. West can teach a new girl to be a good rider now." Renna nodded and slipped her leg off the horn, falling to her feet. She nodded to the trader.

"No need to try anything else. This is the one." Pleased, the man led their chosen mounts to the coach where he tethered them.

Their purchases decided, they went to look at the saddler's caravan. The resourceful soul had followed the horse trader for good reason, and he smiled in welcome as they approached. The girls went to select some properly fitted tack for their new mounts. All the while, Fallswell's coachman remained to oversee their progress and safety. He hung by the coach while they slowly browsed the wares artfully displayed by the mobile saddler. The coachman also conducted the business of payment with the traders while the girls shopped.

As Dae ran her fingers over the soft suede seat of a deep mahogany colored saddle, she felt her skin rise up into little bumps and all around her, the air seemed to thicken. As she turned she found herself facing a ghost. It was startling, to be out in the open, surrounded by people and horses, and to be staring into the face of a dead man. She turned waxen, and Renna gasped.

The young man stood directly before Dae, he wore a greatcoat that fluttered in a nonexistent breeze. A broad brimmed hat sat atop his head. His gloved hands were grasped against his stomach, and he gazed up dourly at her from his bowed head. Although he looked angry and violent, he was devastatingly handsome. He lifted his chin and mouthed silent words at her. Her look of shock and incredulity only frustrated the apparition, so he screamed mute words at her. When she did not respond, he flew into a rage and turned into an enormous blot, before twisting into the ground and vanishing.

"Goodness me! That's a first. What do you think that was about?" Renna blurted.

"Search me," Dae replied in a broken voice.

"Well, this town is as bad as Fallswell with the damned ghosts," Renna declared

"Language, Renna," Dae warned. The girl rolled her eyes.

"I'm riding back on Typhon. I don't know about you." Renna pointed out two saddles to try and sailed towards her newly christened horse with the saddler in tow. Dae returned to the coach for her outerwear, and put it on, still gazing in puzzlement at the spot where the angry ghost had stood. It reminded her of Pip and her cryptic message. She dwelled on it while saddles were chosen, and continued to all the way back to Fallswell.

Returning to the library was Dae's priority the following morning. Renna and Ammette decided to mar the fresh layer of snow by going out for some exercise in the saddle. Dae had to convince them at length that she was not disposed to riding this cold morning, and she would rather continue organizing Ammette's books. She also stressed that the visitors would soon be arriving, and although they were scheduled to arrive later that day, one could not discount the possibility of faster horses or an earlier ship.

The housekeeper had a brisk fire in the hearth when she entered the room, and another spread of tea and assorted refreshments waited on the work table. Dae threw herself into her work. She hoped Pip might melt up onto one surface or another. But for most of the morning all she saw or heard of ghosts was the flicker of one of the blots crossing the room, and a shrieker, possibly the one they called Frek, trying to scare the new, deaf girl Adda in the corridor as she came to refresh Dae's tea.

Adda, bright eyed and cheerful, gave Dae a grin as she changed out the tea pots and presented her with the tea box. "The fat ghost likes me," she said in her unique accent. Deafened by illness as a child, she could speak, but the deafness had given her speech its own pleasant lilt over the years. She could read lips quite well, and was probably the best suited for living and working in this house.

Apparently, the seemingly horrifying manifestation of a shrieker was less frightful if it wasn't accompanied by the spine tingling screams. Adda found them amusing, and Frek was possibly disturbed by her lack of respect of his fearsome nature for he did manifest himself for her more than anyone else since her arrival.

"I've learned one thing since I've come to this place. Ghosts want to be seen and heard. Ammette does not ignore them, but she metes out her notice enough to keep them in line. You are still new here. In a week or two, Frek will go back to his once-daily scream."

"That is too bad," Adda laughed. "I think he is so funny. Popping out, all round and fluffy, from the walls, arms waving…" She demonstrated by bending her arms over her head like tree limbs in the wind. Dae laughed, and thanked Adda. The girl bustled out in her black wool dress and crisp white apron, with a pleasant smile on her face. Frek could be heard following her.

After the brief interruption, Dae poured fresh tea in her cup, and got up to put her newly sorted stack of books onto the next shelf. As she did, the angry spectral man appeared again directly between her and the shelves. She dropped her books in surprise, and cursed in annoyance, giving the ghost a glare as she stooped to pick her books up again.

Her irritated reaction seemed to astonish the ghost. His fearsome air melted into one of being dumbfounded. This time he did not make a silent scream and vanish. He remained rooted to his spot, watching with a black glare, as Dae collected and re-sorted the books and filed them on the shelf. She walked right through him, back to the table, only acknowledging him with a glance while she sat down to sort through her next box.

After a bit, he moved closer, enough so that he stood with the edge of the table cutting into his body. "What is it?" She finally snapped at him. She put down the book she was looking at and stared up at him with a look of great impatience. "If shriekers can make noise, logically you should be able to. Speak, or I shall ignore you henceforth. Ask any of the ghosts in this house, I can ignore the worst of them! I won't play riddles or guessing games with you. I will not be a source of amusement to ease your eternal state."

He looked furious for a moment and then vanished. Dae scoffed in irritation and glowered at nothing. She sighed and went back to work. She drank another cup of tea. She filled another shelf and emptied another crate of books. She broke the crate up with her foot, and added it to the hungry fire. She stooped there a moment, watching the flames consume the wood. She then straightened herself, wiped off the front of her gown and returned to the table.

As she did a wall of blots exploded from the wall, and in doing so, they launched the neatly filed books out into a shower of projectiles. Dae fell onto her knees, and covered her head, using the work table as a shield against the pummeling of falling literature. When the event subsided, she emerged from her crouch, her hands trembling.

Around her, the once improved state of the library was now again in a terrible disarray. There was only one spot not covered in books and debris. It was where she had set up her tea. The only thing disturbed was the sugar pot, which had been toppled, and in the spilled sugar, the words 'dead dead dead' had been scribed by a spectral hand.

Figson Howkes was an undesirable looking character, with a seemingly bland personality that only made him appear less appealing. The girls knew him well, for he had been the family attorney for many years, and took his awkwardness and taciturn nature in stride. He was a thin, bony creature, with a large, sharp nose that dominated his features. His eyes, which were a particularly beautiful shade of hazel, were buried in deep sockets, which were tinted in an unhealthy purple hue. His lank, oily hair hung to his ears. It would be a pleasant coppery red if it weren't plastered to his head with pomade and styled so carelessly. His lips were thin and hardly distinguishable from his face. A sharp chin, bony hands, hunched shoulders and crane legs; this unfortunate man preceded the court's magister into the formal parlor where the ladies had gathered after lunch.

The magister was the opposite in every aspect, to the attorney the girls knew. He was handsome, with fair hair fashioned in a rakish tousle; a controlled carelessness that many youthful men sought to achieve. He wore the finest fashions, carried himself with confidence and his azure eyes were lit up by the fresh, lovely faces of the girls. After being introduced by Figson, he bowed deeply, and embraced the hand of each lady, starting with Ammette.

"Magister Lesk, you are welcome," Ammette flushed like a young woman.

"I thank you. You have a bit of a ghost problem I see," he declared with a humorous grin. Figson mumbled '*genius observation,*' under his breath and sat down where Dae gestured. Dae heard it, and hid her smirk. She watched the attorney shift about and fidget in irritation as the Court Magister ingratiated himself to the women. Renna was particularly talkative and smiling. Dae found something to distrust in the man's easygoing air.

"Oh, don't let the spirits in this house bother you. We have grown accustomed to them ourselves. In fact, we visited rhododendron hall just this morning, Aunt and I, and the shadethers are shockingly thin there. The place felt almost hollow and barren without the spectral activity."

"No ghosts at all?" He replied in surprise.

"Not one," Renna replied decisively.

"I won't say that it is strange. My home does not have ghosts," he muttered. "Some say that home is not a home without some legacy of its past in it. I am not sure I agree. I say, though, in all my days I've never seen a place *this* haunted before."

"I suspect that the reason this house is here is because of a crooked land owner bribing a crooked etherman to flub his shadether land-survey ;so what was otherwise useless land could be sold to the first fool that comes along," Figson snorted.

"Possibly," Ammette replied. "But neither I, nor the girls I find, are so faint of heart that we cannot make a home of this place. It is a good home. The ghosts may be many, but there are none with unkind intentions, and when things are quiet they usually are too. Visitors agitate them, in time they will settle down."

"Our home with our parents had no ghosts," Dae suddenly interjected.

"That's because it was built on a lot with thin shadethers." Figson told her.

"Yes," she concurred. "Although father did say that the house in which we were born had a ghost or two of its own. I only saw ghosts a few times before I came here. It took some getting used to here. But Aunt was excellent at showing us how to treat them so they respect us as residents rather than see us as intruders."

"Myes…" Mr. Lesk replied distractedly, as if he wasn't listening or he was waiting for her to finish so he could speak. He had his chin tucked into his collar and cravat, exposing it suddenly. "You do know the purpose of our visit?"

"You are to interview us, for the case against our parents." Renna said this with no shortage of spite, which seemed to come out of nowhere for only seconds before she was gushing over the visitor.

"This is less a deposition as it is more a character assessment," he said in an overly assuring voice. Imelda and Shisk began to scream and wail far off, halting his words. He looked about in alarm as the voices, chilling and shrill, grew nearer and nearer. Both burst into the room through the hearth, and shot across the space. Two small blots accompanied them; the twins, and they spiraled behind the shriekers flinging small objects about the room.

The ladies were monuments of calm and disinterest. Dae picked up her glass of port and sipped while a small book whizzed past her ear. Renna sat impassively with her hands on her lap, looking with suspicion at the magister. Figson sat stiff, eyes wide; relaxing only after the ghosts had passed through and finished their mischief.

"What we fail to understand is how this is intended to assist our parents, considering that you represent the prosecution?" Renna continued, speaking to a Magister that had turned waxen.

"Madame, you just stated that there were no apparitions of unkind intentions in this house. Those were howlers. They are not passive things. Not to mention that their presence guarantees that this is a prime spot for Terrors," the Magister blurted. "I hope you were not being dishonest with us!" The deviation from the topic took everyone by surprise. The Magister looked positively accusing when he roared these words at Ammette. The lady did not appreciate being spoken to so brusquely, or accused of dishonesty.

"We have no violent ghosts here," Ammette snapped. "The twins are just mischief makers, following a pair of vociferous ghosts that are no more harmful than kittens. There are no Terrors in this house, Magister, I assure you. And I certainly have *not* been dishonest as you so unkindly said." She looked angry. "The spirits in this place, like all spirits, dislike intruders. They will do what they must to get your attention, and strike fear in you. I cannot be responsible for the fact that you are letting them do just that!"

"Those were howlers, certainly NOT kittens!" he replied in severe irritation. Ammette's cheeks reddened.

"Mr. Lesk," Aunt Ammette enunciated through stiff lips, "I have been here going on four years, and I haven't seen any evidence of a Terror. Not a mote. My *howlers* as you call them are nothing more than noise wrapped in an apparition. The only harm they are capable of is to my monthly bill from the ceramicist. I *won't* have you sowing fear in this house, do you hear me? Nor will I permit a guest under my roof to speak to me with such disrespect." Neither of the girls had ever seen their great aunt so flustered and angry. She stood. "You may resume your discussion with the girls this evening. I beg you will leave us, gentlemen." Figson stood and bowed, touching the magister's arm to prompt him to follow. The taller man launched onto his feet, buttoning his frock coat huffily.

"The interviews will take place tomorrow," Mr. Lesk blurted stiffly. The women gazed at him impassively as he gathered himself and followed Figson out of the room.

"I hope Imelda spends the night in his room," Renna said angrily. "So rude!"

Dae was unsure what to make of the discussion about violent ghosts. She had just been threatened by one. If Ammette was right, this ghost was new to the hall. Perhaps it had followed her home. But she suspected it had really followed her to Bembly and it was the one Pip had warned her about. She kept her lips closed, and sat down. Sensing Ammette's unease, Ortner materialized over her head. His smoky roils looked more agitated than usual. The ghosts all sensed something was awry.

"I can't wait until they're gone," Ammette confessed. The girls nodded solemnly and all three fell into a tense silence while around them, blots and shimmers of spirits restlessly gathered.

Dae was startled to awareness by the increasingly violent shaking of her bed. She nearly fell onto the floor scooting out of it, and stumbled to her feet on the smooth, worn rug of her sleeping chambers. The bed shook a few more times and then fell deathly still. It was past midnight, judging by the position of the moons in the sky. She measured her breathing and calmed herself, cursing bitterly under her breath in a most unladylike manner as she clutched her night gown closed under her chin. All around her, little blots were stirring.

"What is it?" she asked, gazing around at the inky forms darkening the already darkened room. The low fire shed only minimal light into the space, but it was enough to see the wash of black brought by the presence of many ghosts. "What do you want of me at this hour?" she snapped. She stood, shivering from the shock of being thrown out of her warm covers, wide-eyed and bleary; tracking what movement she could in the darkness. What she saw was a culmination of the blots. They drifted together into a large smudge of nothing, a black, empty hole in the world, where no light could pass.

It was then, that the hole of darkness began to resolve into the effigy of her angry gentleman. "I am ignoring you," she warned him before his form fully took shape. The ethereal glow of the quiet ghost began to define its features and most of his torso. His arms and legs faded into the black of the blots. He gazed at her balefully, and the floor started to shake. She cocked her head and furrowed her brow.

"Are you a Terror?" The blots grew agitated at this question and began to flit around the figure in the darkness. She frowned deeply and her eyes grew angry. "You are, aren't you?" The ghost shook his head once. His hand reached up and his finger pointed at Dae; or through her. She could not be sure.

"I'm fairly sure I'm not a Terror," she replied with a touch of snideness. She gripped her gown tighter under her chin. "Who are you? And why are you following me? Bothering me? Why?" The ghost stared at her again.

Dae took in his form. He must have cut a fine figure in life, she surmised. He was so handsome. He was refined in the shape of his face, and intriguing in the depth of his eyes. There was an intriguing air about the way he looked at her. There was a mix of hate and underlying rage. She had no idea what to make of it. "Until you figure out how to properly communicate what you want of me, I cannot continue to tolerate these cryptic visits. If you cannot work on a way to express what you wish to me in a rational way, I will pretend you do not exist, like so many people do with ghosts. Now unless you have something constructive to say, besides threatening messages written in spilled sugar, please go away!"

And with that, he did. The cluster of spectral shapes exploded away in all directions from the form, and it dissipated. As a parting gift, her mirror shattered and the shards exploded towards her. She fell to her knees and hunched into a ball, the glass raining over her. When all was still, Dae resolved to decipher this mystery. In the morning, she would take immediate action.

Little did Dae know that her early escape from the house atop her sidesaddle created a stir with the guests. The Magister and the attorney were displeased as the interviews were to begin that morning after breakfast. Dae did not consider the interviews to be all that dire, and Renna would be there to compensate for her absence. She rode towards the village of Sedge, a five mile trek across the icy, rutted wheat fields, down into a valley that followed the curve of a broad river, over a stone bridge and into the tiny hamlet which was at present, beautifully swathed in snow.

Aere, her new mare, took this journey with great alacrity, stepping high over the snow, her nostrils wide and snorting, billowing out steamy clouds scented of molasses and grain mash. Dae was swaddled in her heaviest woolen habit, with a navy blue, fur trimmed hooded cape, her hands bound in soft rabbit fur lined gloves. The biting air was bracing, but refreshing. The road had been cleared in the small village, and a few people were out and about. She rode up to a tall, slightly crooked daub and wattle building with precipitously cantilevered upper stories, and verified the directions that Adda had given her, written on a piece of parchment.

Adda had discovered the mess of mirror glass early that morning when she came to stoke the fire, and asked Dae what had happened. Dae, unsure about confiding this event to her sister or her great aunt, told Adda what had happened, and asked her what could be done. The girl's response was surprisingly accepting and rational.

"You need to hire a ghoster, Miss Dae. I know of a good one." The girl proceeded to give Dae directions which she scribbled down on a scrap of paper. She resolved address the problem at once; and was on her horse as soon as she was dressed and before the rest of the household was up and about.

"This is it, Aere." She lifted her right leg over the fixed horn and slid out of her saddle; her boots crunching on the thin layer of icy snow that remained after ploughing. She tied Aere to the ring on the plinth by the stoop, and in a train of hems, she sailed up the steps and pulled the bell. Inside it rang loudly. A dog barked and there was a responding bark from its owner to shut its damned dog mouth. The door was gruffly yanked open and she was looking into the astonished face of a man who had just rolled out of bed.

He held her gaze for a long moment, studying her freckled, pretty face, his hand unconsciously rasping across his unshaven jaw. "I'm sorry to be a boor, sir, but it is cold. May I come in?" Dae asked as politely as she could. The man furrowed his brow and shook his head as if being startled back to reality, and then wordlessly stepped back and opened the door for her to pass. In a nightshirt, a banyan that had been hastily thrown onto his arms, and under breeches with no shoes or stockings, he followed her inside after closing the door. She was greeted enthusiastically by a silver colored bird hound, whose entire body wiggled in delight to meet her. His glistening eyes and excited pant made her miss her dogs, and she knelt before him to cuddle him and scratch his ears.

"If you don't mind, I'll go and make myself presentable," the man finally spoke, watching her from his lofty height. She pushed back her hood and looked up at him, nodding. He glanced at her briefly in puzzlement, and then disappeared through a low archway, where he could be heard climbing creaky stairs. He had led her into an informal parlor furnished in shabby, aged furniture and dark, masculine draperies. The walls were both paneled in dark woods and plastered, adorned with a peppering of fine oils and a couple of especially bright and beautiful watercolors that seemed out of place in the heavy, low ceilinged room. She petted the dog a bit more, and saw herself to a squashy old wingback by the fireplace. The fire had long fallen into coals, so she took it upon herself to revive it. The supplies were present in a large basket by the fender. She stripped off her cloak and gloves, and put them over the back of the chair, and knelt by the fireplace. The dog approached and sat down beside her to observe as she stoked the coals and added kindling.

She did not hear the gentleman return, she only felt his eyes on her. When she straightened and wiped her hands on her skirts, she found him leaning in the doorway, watching her. Still in a banyan, he at least now wore long trousers and carpet slippers on his feet. He'd tamed his wild hair with a tapestry box hat. His arms were crossed and he stared at her with eyes the color of evergreens.

"I would normally ask what brings you here, but I already know," he grunted, shaking his head.

"Yes. I am haunted by a terror. My abigail said you could help me." He furrowed his brow and blinked, as if incredulous.

"Haunted by a terror? No you are not. You're a Revenant, my dear. You're being hunted by a wraith." He said this matter-of-factly, dismissing her previous statement with a casual gesture and a bit of an impatient snort.

"I'm sorry, what?" She asked, confused.

"A Revenant. You died. You live again. You are an aberration, and the shadether wants you back." She stood there, gape-mouthed for a long pause, not understanding him. He stepped forward and grabbed her wrist brusquely, twisting her hand so that her palm faced up. He pushed back her cuff to reveal the tender skin of her wrist and the fine lacework of blue veins just below the surface. He pushed his thumb hard into her skin. She whimpered, afraid. He then let go and pointed at her wrist. The spot where his thumb had been was white, the color slowly washing back. The white skin was etched with two small intricate figures, which remained flushed. They looked like glyphs. They were quickly blended away by the return of the blood.

"The mark of a deathwitch. You were resurrected, my dear. You are not natural to our world or tolerated by the shadethers."

"How could you know?" She gasped, her eyes glossing over, the confusion and shock seeping over her like the cold. Her eyes shifted as she searched for some clue to all this in her mind.

"You came here for the services of a ghoster, did you not? I know what I see. You are surrounded by the residue of the shadethers. They will forever follow you. The wraith wants you to go back. It's what they do. If you are anywhere where the veil between our worlds are thin, it will find you." Her disbelieving stare fell upon him and she could only shake her head.

"It isn't often that the Revenant does not know what it is."

"I am not an *it*," she snapped. He sighed and gestured for her to sit.

"Most revenants arrange for their resurrections. They wake up with no memory of their death. The resurrectionist remains present to inform them of what has occurred. That happens in *most* cases. Sometimes not. May I ask your name?"

"Dae," she replied in a broken voice. "My name is Dae." He nodded and stalked across the room to a large breakfront. He knelt and opened a cabinet at its base, and riffled things about in it. He slammed the door closed and returned with a strange device. Made of what looked like gold and a bluish metal, it was a clutch of circles with various lenses of different colors embedded in different moving parts. Some glass had a pearlescent wash over the surface; others had figures etched into them. He toggled and fiddled with it for a moment, moving little parts here and there while Dae, now seated, nervously scratched his dog's ears. He then lifted it up and between her face and his, stooping in front of her, and adjusted various lenses until he sighed, and clucked his tongue.

"Sundern spells. You are nascent," he rambled, pausing. "Hmm… Interesting." Dae's confusion was further increased by the fact that she could not stop staring at his lips. They were unusually beautiful. His dark hair and rugged good looks were not helping. How she could be thinking these things at this very moment mystified her. She flushed in embarrassment and dropped her eyes. He toggled bits of the instrument and then slid new lenses into place. "Now that's beautiful," he said absentmindedly.

"You are a most artful creation Miss Dae," he concluded, dropping his hand with the device and straightening. "As close to perfect as I've ever seen. You are newly created. Your deathwitch markings will fade away over time, but anyone with ghoster skills will see your shadether residue. Not all ghosters are easy about revenants like I am. You could be marked, even detained if you travel off the great isle. Some places believe the resurrected to be abominations." Her color drained.

"What of the wraith? Am I forever to be plagued by it?"

"The simple solution is to live where there are little to no shadethers."

"That's impossible. You just told me I am in danger elsewhere."

"Where are you living now?"

"Fallswell..." He barked out laughing before she could finish, and slapped his thigh.

"Ahh that's rich," he sighed good-humoredly. He reached and scratched the back of his head. "I can help with the wraith. Your other ghostly friends will, well, continue to dote. They sense your familiarity. If you would like to wait, I will dress and grab a bite and accompany you to the hall of spirits," he smiled broadly stating the last three words, having a laugh at the expense of Fallswell. "Or," he continued, "you can go and I will follow."

"I'll wait," she sighed.

"Care for a bite and some tea?" he asked as he exited, pausing at the door. She nodded numbly and leaned back into the chair. The dog rested his head on her thigh. She petted him gently, fighting back tears.

Dae stared blankly ahead, unable to wrap her mind around the revelation. Meanwhile, Mr. Drouwd cheerfully rode alongside her on a heavy old breed horse, his green eyes sparkling with interest and questions. Hatter, the dog, his lustrous silver coat shining in the bright, cold sun, loped along with them, grinning as dogs do when free and happy.

"What brings you to Fallswell of all places?" he asked. She glanced at him from the shade of her hood and told him her tale.

"My sister and I had no place else to turn," she concluded. "So here we are."

"Hm," he shook his head. "Bad luck, for you. This area is shot with shadether clouds denser than many other places in the empire.

You are fortunate on one end though, and that is because of this unusual occurrence, people here are mostly hardened to ghosts and ghostly activities. *Mostly.* Your life here would be easier than if you were to live somewhere where the spirit world is rarer and more fearsome to those that encounter it." She nodded. "As long as you avoid the odd ghoster with an undue dislike of crossers." She looked at him questioningly. "Oh, that's a ghoster term for revenants." She nodded, tight lipped and brushed some locks from her eyes.

"Was it a lover that brought you back?"

"I have no lovers," she replied. "I am unsure. I suspect it was my parents, which would explain their detention."

"That would. But their trial is a sign that there is room for doubt. And one of them would surely have to be a deathwitch to be guilty of resurrecting the dead. There are ways of detecting a deathwitch. The courts would already know if your parents are guilty or not."

"Unless they paid someone to do it."

"Ah yes. Them there would be the matter of identifying their agent."

"They would still be found guilty," she concluded. Mr. Drouwd pursed his lips sympathetically and then nodded.

"Why did they not detain me then? I am an aberration."

"Well, not all governments punish people for being torn back from the shadethers; it is not always their doing. It appears that only one or two people know of your state, Miss Dae. Your existence is not the crime. What brought you into existence is. They sent you away to protect you, surely, and your family. From the knowledge of it. Not even you were told what your parents' crime was." She nodded again.

"Your sister must know something. She would remember your death. Your return." Dae pursed her lips, and started to shake her head.

"Renna is a terrible liar. She cannot keep a secret. If we were ever apart I would say she simply did not witness my death or the resurrection you speak of. But we are rarely away from the other, aside from being in different rooms each day." Dae felt her skin going cold. "If this is all true and the Revenant does not recall its death, then I can only surmise that we both died. And the longer I think on it, the more I am convinced it happened when we both became ill with Avasanne, while mother was at Rellemstad. We were so ill, we were comatose. But we considered ourselves lucky to have survived." Her voice faded as she spoke, the last words a whisper. "But we didn't, did we? We died."

"Likely so," Mr. Drouwd retorted. She hid inside her hood, the pall of this revelation descending more heavily upon her. Together with the dog at their heels, they returned to Fallswell in possession of the truth.

Dae did not brook questions about her guest. Renna, who was generally easy going, had been tense and emotional upon their arrival in the later hours of the morning. Dae met her sister's worried gaze with one of her own, for entirely different reasons.

"Where have you been?" Renna blurted. She was waiting by the rear entrance where Dae and Mr. Drouwd entered from the stable. She looked at Mr. Drouwd with open puzzlement.

"Seeking help from a ghoster. That ghost we saw at Bembly... it's been haunting me. It threatened me," Dae replied. Renna frowned.

"Why did you not tell me?"

"I did not think it a problem, until it shook me from my bed last night and shattered my mirror." Renna sighed, her anger dissipating a bit.

"I have been subject to inquisition all morning about you; your habits; and comments about your supposed inconsiderate nature. They were to hold interviews this morning, and your absence caused all sorts of discord. He was determined to interview you first, you see, and that your absence has interrupted the process. The Magister would not listen to Mr. Howkes. He suggested that they start interviewing me, and wait for you but the Magister would not have it. Instead, he threw a fit, and shouted at me, and accused you of bad manners and all sorts of things. Mr. Howkes had to shout at him to remind him that he was making a spectacle of himself. He is such a rude man!"

"Mr. Drouwd, this is my sister Renna. Renna, this is Mr. Drouwd," Dae mumbled, removing her cloak as she entered the home, and hanging it on a peg. She took her guest's garrick and hat and hung them next to hers. Renna finally acknowledged Amdreus with a sheepish nod, and led her back to the drawing room where Dae and her guests were met with a grumpy magister and a family attorney who looked exhausted. The magister insisted on taking her into the library immediately to interview, and he succeeded in doing so.

Mr. Howkes immediately frowned. As he did whenever a man entered the circle of the ladies. Especially a well looking fellow like Mr. Drouwd. He bowed stiffly when the introductions were made, and was loth to leave him behind. Before he exited with Dae and the magister, he slipped into the office where Ammette was quietly working on her correspondence and household accounts.

"Who is this man?" Figson snarled at Ammette, who was busying herself with her daily tasks. She looked at the gawky attorney and frowned. "A young local man. A ghoster. His name is Amdreus Drouwd. I've met him before, when I first came to Fallswell. He came by to offer his services, to remedy any issues with terrors or worse. As these are gentle ghosts, I did not require his services. He's a decent young man."

"What is she doing going out to fetch him, then? Without your leave no less?"

"Mr. Howkes, why do you ask me? I do not have a window into her mind. I can only guess her motivations." Ammette shook her head and returned to her scribbling.

"Ghosters are dangerous people," Figson mumbled. He then exited the office, through the glass paned doors, and entered the parlor where Renna and Mr. Drouwd sat, while Dae and the Magister prepared for the interview. Figson had to join them, but he did not wish to leave the ghoster with Renna. He had no choice, and exited in a visible huff.

"Tell me, Miss Dae; are you at present engaged, or spoken for?"

"Magister, I don't understand why this would be relevant to…"

"Answer the question, Miss Dae," Figson mumbled irritably.

"No."

"Why not? Most ladies of your age are usually entertaining these ideas, at least. No special young men cross your mind?" She glanced at Figson, who merely nodded.

"No. I... I am not like that. I am not flirtatious or outgoing. My mother found it frustrating, for she hoped for us both to marry well. I have always thought that if there is someone there for me, I won't meet him in the conventional way, because he, like me, won't care for conventional things. Neither my sister or I have any urgent desire to chase uninteresting men to please everyone else." Figson smirked and bowed his head. The magister nodded once and looked at the papers on the table before him. Around them, the work of organizing books was suspended in a state of disarray. The hastily gathered stacks of books had only just been collected from around the room to be reorganized. The sugar had been cleaned up, and the carpet swept of other bits and bobs that the spectral tantrum had dislodged. It bothered Dae that she could not continue with the library until they left.

"So your sister has no secret lovers?" Dae merely laughed through her nose.

"Renna couldn't keep a secret of anything. She's an open book."

"Your father had someone lined up for you, I believe. A Mr. Kallenback..."

"Mr. Kallenback was my father's business associate, who expressed an interest in me. My father thought him too old, and I was apt to agree. He did ask permission, and my father told him as a friend that he could not deny him the right to ask. I declined, naturally, much to father's relief. I was careful to do so kindly as not to jeopardize the relationship the two shared in business, although he did not take it well."

"Mr. Kallenback claims otherwise. He said you agreed and your father objected. Now that your father is detained, he hopes you will reconsider." Dae looked at the Magister with her face twisted into a look of incredulity, and Mr. Howkes sat up straight in his chair.

"I beg your pardon, but that is a lie!"

"An opportunist! Imagining that without a family or fortune that she would indeed change her mind!" Figson barked. "What has this anything to do with the case, Magister?"

"Everything is relevant, Mr. Howkes! Especially if her father's honesty and credibility are in question. Is Mr. Kallenback a liar then? To what end? To discredit an already discredited man?"

"No, Magister, to get his ham hands on a beautiful, elegant, sweet young woman which he openly desired in spite of his age being much too advanced for such a young lady," the attorney growled. "You forget that I was the family's attorney for many years. I assisted Mr. Evlan with his business, and I am well familiar with Mr. Kallenback's fascination with Miss Dae. He first met her at a carding evening, and recently widowed, he delighted in her considerate and polite attentions. I recall most clearly his delusions. Arrick wouldn't have it," he spoke Dae's father's name with such familiarity it made Dae's eyes tear up. How she missed her father.

"Did he pursue you aggressively?"

"He sent gifts. Hampers from his country estates, a writing slope that I still possess. Trinkets and the like. He never characterized these gifts as anything romantic, but I confess perhaps my naïveté might have prevented me from seeing it as anything more than kindness. Father never alluded to his interest in me, except when he told me of his allowing Kallenback to propose. He told me to answer him with honesty, that my choice and my happiness were paramount. I believed him. I declined knowing my father would not hold it against me."

"What happened when you declined?" Dae dropped her gaze, and shifted uncomfortably. Figson also looked perturbed.

"I told him that I was surprised by his interest, and I fibbed and told him I was flattered. I then kindly explained that I was too young still to settle on the idea of marriage. I told him I thought I might eschew the traditional life it to pursue a life as a Zillig…"

"Is that true? You considered that?" The Magister looked astonished.

"No. I admire Zillig women, but I am not suited to walk in the footsteps of men. I lied, I admit. I did not want him to be hurt by my rejection. I did not want to harm the business relationship he and my father shared. I told him that I wasn't ready for the decision about marriage or choosing a life of career as a Zillig. I figured I could postpone him until he found someone else to pursue."

"His reaction?" Dae paused.

"He hit me."

"I beg your pardon?"

"He raised his arm and hit me with the back of his hand. The force of it threw me from my chair." Her voice wavered. "I saw stars behind the lids of my eyes, and the pain was unbelievable. Father heard the commotion and entered the room; they exchanged blows. Mr. Karm and Levnik came in and separated them. Mr. Kallenback was escorted from our house and the militia was summoned." Figson reached out and patted Dae's hand. She gave him a weak smile. The tears welling in Dae's eyes threw the Magister off. He sat back and cleared his throat.

"I have no reason to lie or discredit this man," she added. "This is what happened. He never returned. He cut all ties with my father's concern, much to my regret. But father never begrudged me for it. Even with the loss of income from the incident. Father soon found another shipper and all was well again. I have been loath to interact with our family's society since, in fear of attracting another such a man."

"What was Renna's reaction to all this?"

"This was when I was but 16, Magister," his eyebrows shot up at this assertion; "Renna is four years my junior. She was interested only in her new dapple pony and first colored silk dress at the time."

"I see." The magister's hands reached for a stack of papers, which he tamped even before rolling them up and filing them into a tube. "We will continue this on the morrow Miss Dae; I think we have had enough of the Kallenback matter. We will move onto another when we resume. Please do not leave without notifying us again." She nodded in assent and he got up and exited the room.

"Are you holding up?" Figson asked. She smiled tersely and stood.

"I've made it thus far, Mr. Howkes." He graciously bowed and then opened the door for her to slide out of the library before him. She waited for him to shut the door. "How long is this to go on, Mr. Howkes?"

"I honestly don't know," he replied. She turned away and returned to the parlor to find the ghoster, the attorney at her heels.

"I apologize for the long wait, Mr. Drouwd. This business could not wait apparently," Dae grumbled irritably. Mr. Drouwd only nodded and focused on her reddened eyes.

"At the risk of being forward, Miss Dae, are you unwell? You appear as if you have been weeping," he ventured.

Figson snorted through his nose and his mandibles rippled. The Magister glanced at the newcomer briefly and then sat, throwing out his tails before settling. He crossed his legs and shook out a periodical, putting himself behind it. Ammette remained sequestered in her offices, and could be seen writing behind the glass doors, with Ortner hovering predictably over her head.

"I am quite well, Mr. Drouwd, I do appreciate your concern," she replied. "Would you care for some refreshment before your survey?"

"No. I think I'm good for now. We can talk about something warm and bracing after I've swept the place." Dae nodded in assent and he stood, tall and handsome. As he did, Imelda came shrieking from another part of the house, but instead of crossing through as usual, the ghost halted at the sight of the ghoster. Her form expanded into a great ball, and it threw out more arms and limbs, her eyes and mouth gaped and she screamed as if she had the voice of a thousand dead in harmony. Everyone blanched, even Ammette in the next room. Ortner blinked out of existence. Renna gasped. But the ghoster laughed at the massive, fearsome apparition and put his hands on his hips.

"Oh, stop, I'm not intimidated by your theatrics!" he blurted. The ghost shrank back to her normal size and then flitted away in silence. "Well," he said, removing a small pad of paper and a pencil from his frock coat pocket, "one fright specter," he said while writing it down. "Shall we go look for some more?" With a nod, Dae led him out of the room and into the house. Renna, unable to stomach being in the same room, exited without leave. Mr. Howkes was tempted to follow the ghoster and Dae, but instead remained rooted in his seat, glowering.

"The shadether is particularly dense in this area. To this day, I cannot fathom why anyone would build a home here. There is just no peace."

"That is true," Dae conceded. "It is constant. Even when they're quiet, they're not. But you get used to it."

"Yes. As a resident of Mahalav one has little choice on the matter. The shades are a part of life." Dae glanced at Amdreus and sighed shakily.

"I confess I am at a loss as how to feel about my state. I feel as I always have. The same. How am I supposed to feel about it?" She asked. He stopped in the long corridor of the south wing and mirrored her confusion. A shake of the head and a shrug were his initial response. He then rubbed the back of his neck and twisted his elegant lips.

"There is a physical difference. Your body is a fabrication, built by the magic of the deathwitch. Your original vessel is buried where it was when you perished. You are essentially a new person, with your spirit lodged in there. But your memories are unchanged, and we are a sum of those. So you are unchanged, except for the memory of your death. You also now will always be connected to the shadethers. You are still new. As time goes by, if your spirit is not wrenched back into the shades by a wraith, you will form a stronger connection with the dead."

"That's encouraging." Dae continued to walk.

"I'll remedy the wraith situation. We can explore other ways of finding you some peace. With everything else happening, eliminating the one thing we can will make things tolerable." Dae paused again and looked at him in earnest.

"Thank you." He gazed at her in return with a whimsical smile.

"You are most welcome. Come, let us find this ghost of yours."

Explaining to Ammette why Dae went to a ghoster was another issue. With the guests always present, it took having to follow her great aunt to her bedroom that evening to secure the privacy she required. Once Ammette was comfortable in her night clothes, she sat down at the hearth in her apartments with Dae, and the girl finally divulged the whole truth. From the apparition to the fact that she was a Revenant. Ammette quietly listened.

When Dae concluded her missive, Ammette sipped her herbal tea, and Ortner as if on cue, appeared beside her. "Dear girl, I know about your resurrection."

"How?" Dae replied in astonishment. "Did someone tell you?"

"You don't live in a houseful of ghosts and continue in ignorance of such things. They, like you, are family of sorts. They know, so I know." She said this easily. Ortner's tendrils gently stroked the top of Ammette's arm. "Ortner has been very concerned as the density of the shadethers has intensified since your arrival. I had drawn my own conclusions about the situation with your parents." Dae nodded.

"I dare hope this does not change your opinion of us," she said. Ammette chuckled.

"Nonsense. I'm an eccentric old woman who willingly lives in the most haunted residence on this great isle. You only fit better into my world as revenants than you would if you weren't." She paused and looked at Dae. "I would tell Renna with care. Poor thing might not be so stoic as you are."

"Mr. Drouwd has helped me put it into perspective."

"On that subject I wish to offer you advice. Mr. Drouwd is a fine fellow, but I have heard he was once engaged to be married and without good reason, he severed the agreement in a most dishonorable way with the young woman. He is a first son of a rich father, and because of this he lost everything. His father disowned him. I would take care about him. He is likely some sort of rake."

"I appreciate your concern. I highly doubt there is risk of romance, Aunt. I am but a ghost in a manufactured body. What sensible man would want to connect himself to that?" Dae could scarce hide the lament of her words.

"We are all ghosts in vessels, my dear. The manner in which our bodies are made is largely irrelevant," Ammette said dismissively. "Do you know why some places have more shadethers than others?" Dae shook her head.

"The shades are created when a dead person is resurrected. When their essence is called across the voids, there is a permanent scar made in the fabric of our world and that of the shadethers. This isle, for thousands of years, practiced the ancient religion, and what we now call deathwitches and revile, were once revered and worshipped as Druid priests. Resurrections were common on Mahalav. What were once sacred places of resurrection are now the places where the shades are so strong; they seem to be gathering the dead in droves. Fallswell might have once been the foundation of a temple. It is no wonder the spirits of the Fallswell family remain in such numbers."

"I did not know this," Dae muttered in amazement.

"Few people do. The study of the spectral world is not popular, and those that do know are the ones most marginalized by society. Like the deathwitches."

"You know a great deal…"

"Your great uncle was a deathwitch. Of course nobody knew but I. He helped me to see and understand the language of the dead. It made me uniquely suited for this house. And you ladies are especially suited as well. You are part of it now." Dae sighed and slumped into her chair, gazing remotely at the golden light cast by the flames.

"With what the magister is doing, it seems more certain we will always remain here," Dae retorted.

"They did what they did. Out of love, surely. I cannot be sure what can be done for them now." Ammette added. "They seem to be locked into their guilt. The magister is now merely seeking the instrument by which they committed the crime. Your resurrectionist."

"Indeed. They are leaving no stone unturned."

"Go to bed dear. Get some rest. Your interviews continue tomorrow. The sooner they complete them the sooner they will be gone. Your friend the ghoster will return tomorrow and hopefully trap the wraith." Dae nodded, stood and embraced her aunt. She gently passed her fingers through Ortner's arm.

"Goodnight."

Renna took ill the next morning. At least, that was the excuse. In truth, she was heaped on her bed where she'd flung herself, sobbing her misery into her pillows as Dae and Ammette remained close-by and sympathetic. When the sobbing began to abate, Dae proceeded to explain in detail what was developing, and why the magister was truly there.

"How does he expect us to know? If we have no memory of it?" Renna blubbered. "Oh, I wish mother and father had let things be," she wailed. "Look what they must endure now for what they have done." She threw her face afresh into the pillow and wept bitterly. Ammette managed to get her off the bed. Handling her tenderly, she pulled her up and led her to the chair, tucking a blanket around her legs and cooing to her. Dae watched as her doting aunt served Renna some hot tea as the girl languished in the chair by the window. A bit of time passed in quiet. Dae sat down next to Renna and they stared out the window. The sisters watched both Figson and the magister go for a walk in the park, both left with nothing to do since Renna had barricaded herself into her room. "I hate that magister," Renna blurted at the sight of him.

"I think he wishes to sift through what we do remember, to see if a suspect resolves from the mess of our illness and our apparent deaths," Dae ventured. Renna's bloodshot, bleary eyes took her in, and she fell into a fresh bout of sobs. A noise outside alerted Dae, and she stood and peered out of the far window with the view of the driveway. She saw Mr. Drouwd approaching on his large horse with Hatter bounding at his hocks. She sighed quietly in relief and turned to her aunt.

"Mr. Drouwd is here." Ammette nodded quietly and rubbed Renna's back. Ortner, not keen on weeping and sobbing girls, was nowhere to be seen. No ghosts were present for Renna's emotional reaction to the news of her death and resurrection. Dae emitted another sigh and picked up her hems, moving purposefully to the door. "I will be back when he is done, if you are still in here by then."

Dae was at liberty to receive Mr. Drouwd without interference. She left her sister to her aunt's care. She was looking forward to resuming the walk of the great house with him, listening to him murmur as he catalogued the various spectral apparitions they encountered as they explored.

Mr. Drouwd was in a black mood when he entered the house. He greeted Dae with a hard bow, and his furrowed brow and rippling jaw softened a bit at the sight of her freckled face and wide, beautiful eyes.

"Good morning, Mr. Drouwd," Dae said in almost a whisper. "Are you unwell?"

"Hm. I'm well enough. Just some private irritations that have followed me to Fallswell this morning. I promise to shed them as soon as I have some hot tea." Hatter squeezed past him and bounded into the house as if it were his own.

"I think I can arrange that," Dae replied with a soft smile.

"Any sign of your wraith?" he asked gruffly. She shook her head and closed the large door behind him, taking his coat and hat, and leading him into the private drawing room, where she put the items down on a chair and pulled the cord for tea. The dog settled in by the fire, stretching his back and yawning with a whine. She patted his pewter fur, and smiled.

"I have not seen my friend the wraith since the night before last. Seems he is either making himself scarce, or I slept so deeply last night I missed his antics. I did take a bit of my great aunt's soporific tea in order to sleep. I had a great many thoughts making a commotion in my skull, and knowing I had to speak to my sister first thing did not make it easier."

"Well, you should take care of yourself first. I do not live far, and I don't have much work in the winter. It's when the city folk come out to the countryside in summer when business picks up. If we don't catch him today we will catch him tomorrow. No worries." Dae nodded, and sat down.

"It is a surprise to me that you bother with your business at all, Mr. Drouwd. My aunt says you are a titled heir, are you not?" He seemed to darken a bit at the mention, unaware that Dae was manipulating him.

"I have been disinherited," he blurted. Dae raised her brows in curiosity.

"Oh, I see," she whispered. "That is indeed tragic." He shrugged petulantly and crossed his legs.

"I am making a suitable living. I am happy. That is what is most important." Dae sat down on the edge of the chair to his right, her body angled towards him. She gazed at him with sympathy. "My questionable mood upon arrival is related to this subject, for I have had another communication from my mother begging me to relent."

"Of course. I will not presume to ask why you have given up your family, but I cannot lie and say I am not curious."

"Oh, it's common knowledge around these parts. I'm surprised your aunt hasn't told you all of it."

"She might not be aware of the whole story," Dae defended her. She wanted him to tell it from his side, and she did not want to use what her aunt told her to abuse him. He sighed begrudgingly and scooted to the edge of his seat so that their discussion would be more intimate.

"My father, as any rich, powerful man would be, likes to have his way. And when I graduated from university, he was determined to see me married. So, four years ago, he called upon a fellow member of the peerage to hold a coming out ball for his daughter so that we could be properly introduced. Both her father and mine were clearly motivated for this union. Her father feared his beautiful girl would fall victim to a fortune hunter, and wanted most to preserve the pedigree. My father liked that she came with a significant fortune, and saw countless ways to invest it to help us secure our family's assets and legacies. It was in their mind, a match not to be rivaled." Amdreus spoke with no shortage of spite in his tone.

"It was predestined for me to dislike the girl. There would be no doubt…"

"You knew this before you even met her?" Dae gasped. He nodded.

"Yes," he said with alacrity. "Naturally, she was accomplished in all the *expected* ways; painting, drawing, engaging in skillful discourse, tra-la-la-la-ing at the pianoforte; she could even make her own bobbin lace. But her *true* skill was the one she had been trained in from childhood, and that was the art of husband hunting." He sat even farther forward. Dae blushed at his nearness.

"The problem with ladies like her is that once they've secured their quarry and achieved the end of all that grooming, what are they left with? A lifetime of work towards the attainment, and then nothing to prepare them for the acquisition. They are often empty and lost after they've won their prize. Naught but hollow dolls whose entire sense of self is immolated the moment they are promised. After that, all they do is sit and smile, and act as brood mares in expensive gowns. There was no substance to her. This effigy of a woman was not what I wanted. All she did was flick her fan and preen at the mirror. Oh gods, and the creature was as boring as a haystack." Dae barked out laughter and quickly curbed it. She pressed her fingers to her lips and shook her head.

"Sorry," she muttered as the maid entered with a tray of tea. "I should not have laughed." He waved her off and slumped back into the chair. He waited for Dae to mete out the tea from the box into the pot and add the water to steep. Once that was done, they waited for the maid to leave. She poured him a cup, handing it across to him on the saucer, the china clicking pleasantly. He took it and drank it down piping hot.

"I loathed her the moment we were introduced. Simpering, vapid creature with no true conversation. Angling herself just so to catch my eye, flirting with her fan. She was pretty, there was no question of that, but there's a great more to be desired in a partner than golden side-curls and a fine décolletage. I foresaw a future of strategic planning, so as to avoid being anywhere she was. That is no life. I had my education. I was gifted with the ethersenses. Why would I cow to my father's wishes merely to advance his goals? Naturally, my life would have to change, my habits and whatnot. But telling my father no, and being disinherited was the best thing to happen to me. I am responsible for me and for the dog. And I will choose my own partner. One that isn't a puppet." He gazed at Dae when he spoke and she flushed again. "A partner who is aware of who I am, and not concerned about what fortune I do or do not possess."

"Hm. It's a cynical outlook, but one I can understand," Dae replied. "My sister and I have continuously challenged our parents' wishes and recused ourselves entirely of the mating dance that is expected of us. My mother especially hoped to see us well married. But we are too strange, Renna and I. Too single minded. Both determined to find our own paths on our terms. It drove my mother mad," she said wistfully. She suspired. "I can relate." They looked at one another for a long moment, and shared it in silence. Then Mr. Drouwd bent forward, poured himself another cup of tea, drained it, and got to his feet.

"Let's track that bugger down, shall we?" She nodded. As they exited the room, he asked how Renna was, and she related her sister's state as they climbed the stairway to the upper floors. He nodded in commiseration, all the while his eyes wide and alert for spectral movements.

It was another fruitless search. The ghosts, by their very nature, understood what Mr. Drouwd was. Most all of them kept away. They stopped to take some lunch and joined the two guests, Great Aunt Ammette and to everyone's surprise, Renna, whose puffy eyes and pale face removed any doubt of her claims of feeling unwell.

Mr. Howkes and the Magister stood politely when Dae entered the small, informal dining room. Figson openly admired her in her dark, conifer green day gown of linen, with the bold and bright embroidery typical of Garvash, circling the long hem and train, and creeping up the front of the gown to the bodice. Her long sleeves and ruffed neck gave her a serious air that seemed to agree with the attorney; for he offered her a rare smile, which instantly vanished the moment Mr. Drouwd followed her into the room.

"I see we still require ghosting services," he glowered. Dae did not reply and sailed to her chair, where Amdreus helped her to sit.

"Given the volume of apparitions in this place, if given leave to do so, I could have enough here to carry me to retirement. Sadly, the ladies of the house want to keep their ghosts on the most part. I am here for one occurrence in particular," Mr. Drouwd said with good humor. Figson and the Magister froze at the assertion.

"There is a terror then," the magister concluded with a smug smirk, poking his fork at a piece of mutton.

"No. There is a wraith." Mr. Drouwd and Dae had decided to cast away all pretensions now that Renna was informed of everything. There was no reason to continue to foster the guests' notion that the girls were still ignorant of their state. Mr. Howkes blanched.

"Indeed? How? Would it have followed the girls? Could it?" Amdreus sat down and arranged the napkin on his lap, taking a moment to fill his goblet with snow-water. He drank deeply, enjoying the crisp, cold liquid. With a satisfied grunt, he put the cup down.

"Every resurrection spawns a wraith," he said in a tone of puzzlement. "I've mulled over this. There *should* be two. But there are not. Why would that be, I wonder?"

"I don't understand," Renna muttered in a faint voice.

"You should also be haunted my dear. Especially now that you are here, where the door is open for all manner of apparition, from the most harmless shadow to the most violent of terrors."

Dae frowned at her empty plate and served herself of the mutton and boiled potatoes, spooning some of the gravy over her plate. There was a tense silence as she did this.

"Mr. Drouwd has had difficulty in tracing the presence of my specter," she explained. "Normally, a wraith would be more apt to appear and to expose me for what I am. Mine however, seems half hearted at best. Easily sent away."

"He did seem a sorry soul," Renna added. "All bedraggled and morose. He was handsome once, when he lived." Figson's eyes widened, and he froze.

"Huh," Mr. Drouwd interjected with a sound of surprise.

"He has a face?"

"Yes," Dae replied. "Is that relevant?"

"Wraiths are not ghosts of the conventional type; they are not the spirit of a mortal person. Wraiths are products of the shadethers. They are a short of shadow, left behind by the spirit that was removed from the shadethers by resurrection. They do not have faces; they have only malevolence for having been left behind. This changes a great deal for you both."

"What could you mean?"

"How long have you been in residence, if I may ask?"

"Five weeks, give or take," Dae answered, her face filled with curiosity.

"And no wraiths…" Amdreus thought aloud. "And your ghost, you said it created physical manifestations?"

"It wrote in sugar, and shook the bed. It shattered my mirror most violently. Threw books. But I'm not sure it was the one actually accomplishing these things. I think it was controlling the little blots. There have always been blots with this ghost, except when it was out at Bembly. But it made no physical effect on the world then. It merely appeared." The ghoster sighed and shook his head.

"Most curious, Miss Dae. Most curious." He served himself some food and ate. His eyes distant and preoccupied, leaving everyone else want for illumination.

The ladies were subjected to interviews that afternoon. The Magister seemed even more pressed to find the answers he wanted. But Renna was implacable. Her resentment and her sorrow were too much to bear, and being interrogated by the magister whom she now despised was her limit. She was hostile and impatient, and she stormed out in tears when he asked her the same question twice.

Dae wanted to be with the Ghoster, who now wandered the house on his own. He had become reflective and quiet through lunch and told Dae he would be fine searching alone. Her mind was preoccupied with him and with his declaration at lunch.

"Tell me, Miss Dae. How did you come to realize your state of being?"

"You mean that I am a revenant? Just say what it is, Magister, there's no need to coddle me." He frowned uncomfortably, and shifted in his seat.

"I confess I am no enthusiast of the spectral world, Miss Dae. As a child, I endured some traumas involving ghosts and specifically, terrors, I would rather expedite this visit if we could so I can return to a sane place where the shadethers are reasonably faint or completely non-existent. Now, I have been told by your attorney here, I have been treating you with undue hardness, perhaps as a manifestation of my personal prejudice against the spirit world, I cannot truly say. It is possible, as you are now the embodiment of the very thing I cannot bear. I have resolved to be kinder in order to ease this process. Your sister is determined to undermine my efforts, Miss Dae. I hope you will not as well."

"My sister, as well as myself, just discovered that we were dead and then returned to the living world in bodies that are not our own, Magister. I'm sorry this revelation has caused us to behave irrationally, and has inconvenienced you," she replied snidely. He glared at her dourly and cleared his throat. Figson could scarce keep from smiling, so he slid his face down into his tall collar, behind his cravat. His eyes shone with humor and affection.

"Now, there is the matter of a Mr. Kabe," the Magister changed the subject, his baleful expression unyielding. Dae imagined the stay at Fallswell was taking its toll on him. He seemed to grow increasingly dour and irritable the longer he remained. Dae wished there *were* terrors at Fallswell. Then she would be free of this intolerable man. The question he asked however left her wanting. She did not know of whom he spoke.

"A Mr. who?" Her sincere confusion could not be mistaken for purposeful obstruction.

"Kabe, Miss Dae. Kabe." She shrugged and shook her head.

"I know nobody of that name."

"Now that is interesting," he said, making a note on his papers, the quill scratching quite loudly in the quiet library. Dae thought the room needed a clock. A loud, ticking clock. She tried to recall the name. Something seemed familiar about it, but it found no connection to a face or person in her memory.

Just as the Magister was about to speak, the room shuddered and books flew off the shelves. The wall with the fireplace bulged as if turned to soft clay and a horde of ghosts exploded from it, followed by the greenish blue specter that had been haunting Dae. She stood and gasped and then shrieked as the stampede encircled her and lifted her off the ground. Figson leapt to his feet and threw himself into the mire of ghostly bodies, and grasped Dae's ankles, pulling her back. The door burst open and Amdreus appeared in a full rage. He stretched out his arms and the air bent to his will.

"Bloody shades, get off…" He growled through gritted teeth. They encircled the ghost and Dae, whose screams were muffled by the volume of spectral bodies suffocating her. Mr. Drouwd used his powers to tear the shell of small shade ghosts from around Dae. They fled as he shucked them. She was growing weaker with each passing moment. One by one he stripped the ghosts away, until there were only a few gathered closely to the so called wraith, wresting Dae into his being. She had fainted, and hung heavily in their grasp. "There you are you blasted dead bastard…" He grimaced, gripping his fists, the ethers constricted around the apparitions and they dropped Dae. She was caught by Figson, who buckled under her weight and collapsed onto the floor clutching her.

"Dae, dearest girl, speak to me…" he exclaimed. He scrambled to sit up, and pulled her limp form onto his lap. The ghoster wrenched the spirit into the grasp of his powers, and bound him down to the physical room with a spectral tether. The ghost fought against its bindings using the strength of its little ghostly avatars, to no avail. Its rage only intensified. Mr. Howkes stared up at it in horror, his face as pale as a ghost. "Good gracious," he blurted, looking for the Magister who had fled to the other side of the room. The man looked equally horrified. They both turned to look at Amdreus, who looked like a beast as he willed this ghost to submission.

"Don't expel him, Mr. Drouwd. That's Eldus Kabe!" The magister shouted. Figson cursed under his breath and clutched Dae tighter into his arms. "Is it not, Figson? You knew him too!" The magister asked.

"That's him. That's your deathwitch," he replied. He dropped his gaze to Dae's face, his mandibles rippling. The ghoster nodded grimly and reached into his pocket. He withdrew a silver vial. He unstopped the little cork top chained to the neck, and held it aloft. With the other hand he gestured his will to the forces of the ether, and the bound ghost began to dissolve and stream in a misty tendril into the mouth of the vial along with the little ghosts that it controlled. It wasn't long before the whole assemblage was sipped up into the bottle. The ghoster stopped it and stuffed it into his pocket. The bottle rattled inside the pocket, moving with the force of the specter's rage. He then knelt beside Dae, and put his hand over her mouth, pulling it away slowly. As he did, a shadowy mist twisted from her mouth. He pulled harder and extracted the invader. With nobody's leave, he gripped his hand and extinguished the shade from existence.

Dae awoke with a start, sitting upright with a gasp. Her eyes fell upon three faces. Renna, who looked so happy to see her awake; Figson, whose eyes looked both relieved and sad, and Amdreus, whose expression was one she would never wish to forget. She could not mistake the affection and pleasure in his green eyes as he witnessed her awakening. "I wasn't dead again, was I? Why is everyone here? What happened?"

"Your ghost happened," he replied. "I've thought on it, and have come to the conclusion that your wraiths, both of them, were already dispatched. The man that haunts you was a deathwitch, by the way he controls the shades. He could possibly be yours. How your resurrectionist ended up dead is still a mystery."

"I don't know him, Mr. Drouwd. I have no memory of him."

"Nor do I, but the name, Kabe, there is something familiar to it…" Renna added airily. Dae nodded, for she too felt in spite of her not knowing who he was, there was a tug of familiarity to the name when she thought on it. Nobody looked at Figson, whose face darkened at the mention of the name.

"I would make this suggestion to you, Miss Dae as you are the eldest. I recommend you ride with me to Dohmirsey. There we can meet with Lady Fern Aylange. She is one of the few Searchers I know who can help you rebuild your memories of the time before your death. This is only if this is what you want. It will close all the open doors, so to speak, but it could open new ones. There is that risk. It may help, but it could contribute to the evidence against your parents. But I suspect their fates are already decided. It would rid you of any further contact with the royal courts and the magistrates, and answer the personal questions you have." Dae nodded numbly and leaned back into the pillows of the settee upon which she rested. She realized only then that she was in the formal parlor.

"I suspect my dear that the magister will want to accompany you. This is pertinent to the crown's case against your parents. If he goes, I go." The attorney spoke now, his reedy voice tense and concerned.

"I will correspond with the Lady. She is sometimes…" Amdreus paused; "selective about whom she devotes her time. She could choose to have nothing to do with this spectacle. There is no way of knowing until I write her." He stood. "I will go home. I will send a note when I have more information, and the possible visitation date." He pulled on his frock coat. "The magister wants possession of the trapped spirit of Mr. Kabe. He will not allow me to entrust it to Mr. Howkes in spite of it being evidence against the crown's charges. But for now, he remains with me." Dae hadn't noticed he was in his shirtsleeves. She liked that he wasn't always so formal around her. She gave him a quiet nod. He reached out and brushed the top of her hand with his fingers.

"Use the time to recuperate. You were nearly suffocated by a hostile little shade. Your friend here," he patted his pocket, "Deathwitch Kabe, held some powerful sway over the small ghosts. Turned gentle spirits into tiny terrors. Why he wished to harm you is still beside me. But when we visit Lady Aylange, hopefully we can determine why." Dae merely gazed at him.

"Thank you for saving me."

"No thanks necessary. Your aunt will receive a bill." He laughed and stalked out to find Hatter and go home.

BOOK 2
THE PROBLEM OF DEATH

Figson Howkes was a naturally driven man. It was partly due to his character, but also because he had parents who wanted very much for him to achieve greater things in life than they had. Because of this, he spent most of his youth away from his family. He attended an excellent school as a child, while both of his parents worked tirelessly to pay for his education.

He was a shining example of scholastic achievement from the beginning. When his death-skills began to resolve, his mother was delighted, but his father was not, and for a while, it was an issue of contention between the parents. It was finally agreed by both that they would encourage him to take a more conventional path in his studies, but Figson's mother still objected silently. She too had death-skills, and she too had been forced to put them aside for a more reliable livelihood.

Figson's father, a hardworking physician and apothecary, was a practical man, and a force to be reckoned with in spite of his taciturn nature. He was the primary parent for Figson. They had no other children. His mother, a Zillig, worked as a merchant marine captain aboard an elegant clipper called Little Jezebel. His mother wasn't often at home. And with Figson's schooling often a distance away, he hardly saw much of her growing up. His relationship with her could not compare to that with his father.

Ryus Howkes was a passive man. He had a quiescent nature, and a nurturing touch. He loved his son deeply, and wanted only the best for him. When Figson came of age to begin choosing his future livelihood, Ryus was adamant he continue to keep his death-arts ability as only a hobby or an interest. He wanted Figson to pursue law, which on Garvash, was a fruitful occupation, for there were many large businesses, and many large fortunes that required legal assistance. There were several of the world's largest firms on the isle, and even the lowest level attorney earned a better income than a physician.

Figson had graduated from his secondaries and had only just returned home from school. Ryus had gone out and gotten several pamphlets on various universities specializing in law, and Figson had scarce taken off his coat and hat before his father handed them to him. As usual, he began with the familiar lecture, advised him once again against pursuing the death arts, in which Figson had shown a natural talent.

"I know your mother would be angry that I am saying this to you, Figs, but you will *never* distinguish yourself in death arts, boy. Not these days. You will always be carrying the stained title of deathwitch whether you will it or not. And all the things you *could* do that aren't against the law will mean nothing and serve you little if all everyone sees is a resurrectionist."

"Father, you haven't even said hello," Figson sighed, taking the pamphlets from his father. The man was an older version of his son. Gawky and almost unattractive, with a large nose and stringy, silver-touched hair also slicked against his oddly shaped skull.

"I know, I know," Ryus grunted. "Come inside. It's been ages, and all I can do is think of your schooling. Your mother has been warning me to behave but you know when she's away how quickly I forget myself."

Figson followed his father into the small drawing room the family used most frequently. The carpet was threadbare, the furniture squashy and shapeless, the wood worn from use. There was a lived-in, loved feeling to this space. A scattering of personal clutter; books, vials of serums, baskets of projects in mid-progress—it was a comfort to be in the stuffy little room. His father sank down into an old chair that had shaped itself to his body, and he reached over and picked up his long-pipe, stuffing it with herbs.

"I've been thinking about the death arts, father. I was allowed to take some classes on Modern Deathwitchery, and there is a great deal a deathwitch can do that is legal and helpful to society. I could ease people into death, pull the spirits of the nearly dead back, use my abilities to build healing flesh for the wounded even," he argued, putting the pamphlets down on the worn worktable where his mother would sometimes draw. His father dismissed this.

"Nobody likes marked flesh my boy. And as a physician, I know it never lasts long if it's not sustained by something from the shadether inside it. It's a dying trade boy, and with resurrection being a crime punishable by death, you best stick to something less stigmatized and risky. I would never try to force you to do what makes you unhappy, my boy, but I will push you as your father, to do what will best serve you. You deserve a good future. A secure income, something that will attract a good lady who will care for you. You are clever, and the law already interests you. Choose something you like and that sustains you. Then you can pursue what you love as an interest or an art." Figson, only fifteen and still very much motivated to please his parents, conceded with a sigh, sitting across from his father and gazing impassively at him. He was keenly aware of the financial sacrifice they made for his success. He could not disappoint or argue with them. It would be too much.

"So which school do you have in mind, father?"

After a nice quiet summer of rest at home, and a short time spent with his mother, Figson set off from his home and his school to the small island of Trephyn, where he entered university to study law. He entered the school at an immediate disadvantage. Most students were from affluence and influence. Most were reasonably attractive people, with money and manners. They had backgrounds and familiarity. Figson was a nobody. A physician's and Zillig's son, with no riches, no title, and no accoutrements, like a horse and carriage, or fine suits of clothes to wear after classes.

He was also awkward and plain looking. It was immediately apparent, as it had been at his previous schools, that he would suffer for it. He had hoped that with older students, maturity would somehow diminish their desire to target him, but he was disappointed to discover that this was not the case. The moment he set foot into the school and took possession of his shabby little room only a poorer student could afford, he became the recipient of negative attention. The entire first year at university for Figson was rife with bullying and cruel pranks. He was chided for his looks, his poverty and his shapeless clothes. He was tormented for his weakness and his passiveness. But in spite of his social drawbacks, Figson managed to maintain the best marks in his class. He tried very much to keep to himself and avoid attention from the students that desired to make his life difficult.

At the conclusion of that year, he went home and said nothing to his proud father about how difficult it was for him. He only presented his father with his flawless scholastic record so far, and his excellent marks and the pride beaming from his father was enough to sustain him, and to prepare him for the next year amongst his tormenters.

The following year he returned to his little room with the expectation of the same. He put on his robes and box-hat for the first day of class, and with a sigh of resolve, forged into the sea of humanity, sliding unobtrusively through the crowds, dropping his gaze, trying to keep his eyes from making contact with the sharks. He managed, most of that morning, to stay out of trouble. He was feeling the inevitable approaching during the noon dining hour in the refectory, where much of the bullying happened.

He took a seat in a quiet corner of the refectory, and put his attention to eating. There was however, a new element added to this dynamic. Freshly arrived from the nation of Dervra, transferred from the law school there to his, was a lean, dapper fellow with jaunty golden hair and twinkling blue eyes. He had an intense, charismatic air about him. Figson had noticed this fellow in passing, it was difficult not to. He was extremely dashing. He bordered on a dandy, save for the robes partly covering his fine garments. Everyone was noticing him. He was taller than almost all the other students, and his golden colorations stood out from the plain blacks and browns and russets of the southern boys attending the school.

Figson glanced up and caught the golden boy looking at him just as one of his many bullies kicked the chair legs out from under him, sending Figson clattering to the ground. There was a smattering of laughter as Figson tried to grasp whatever shred of dignity he could, and pull himself together. The new fellow, however, strode over in a flutter of robes and without warning, kicked the offender in the crotch with all his might.

"Oh, sorry there man, my foot got away from me! Happens all the time, I'm afraid, apologies," he said with frightening sincerity. The boy had folded himself up on the floor, and was curled around his smashed groin. Figson clumsily got to his feet and picked up the chair. He first looked at the chap writhing on the floor, then to the circle of faces looking on, several of which belonging to more of his tormentors, and then to the new lad, who was shaking his head and twisting his lip at the boy in the ground.

"Pity, pity," he lamented. "My limbs tend to have a mind of their own when they detect assbaggery. Can't stop it I'm afraid. Best keep that sort of thing in check, fellows, or more of that will happen." He pointed to the figure groaning on the floor. The new boy's wiry, strong Northern physique and the challenging glint in his eye was all they needed to know that his flippant air was no joke. The crowd dissipated and the stranger took Figson's elbow and led him away. Figson was all trepidation. He could not suss out this boy's motivation to help him.

"Never mind that crud," he gestured with his chin to Figson's upset lunch on the table. "Let's get food off campus, shall we? I am dying to try some of the local fare. First time at Trephyn, you see." Figson stumbled alongside the tow-headed hero, still wordless. They walked in silence for a while, making their way out of the main building and crossing the yard towards the main gate. Then the boy spoke again.

"Can't stomach bullies. I get downright murderous when I see them. My little brother was born with some disadvantages. When we were at academy as children, I learned to intervene with that sort of thing right off. But it never stopped. There was always someone looking to humiliate him." Figson frowned. "I did what I could but I couldn't always be with him. It wore him down. Destroyed his spirit. To come here and see, that even now with young men our age, it still happens." He shook his head in frustration, his cheeks ruddy red with emotion. Figson let him lead him to the driveway, across the park to the main road. They walked to town. Still tentative and confused, Figson remained pointedly silent, trying to figure out this young man.

The market was in full progress for the day when they arrived in town. He and Figson bought some meat pies and cheese and sat on the edge of the center fountain to eat. They tucked in, watching the people, livestock, horses and robed students pass by. Figson ate, unsure what to say to this young man. He then looked at him awkwardly and gave him an uncomfortable smile. The golden boy returned the smile with one of ease and confidence.

"What's your name?" he finally asked; his mouth full of half chewed food. He noisily sucked his fingers after cramming the last bit of pie into his mouth, and wiped them dry on the front of his robes.

"I am Figson Howkes," the thin, red-haired boy replied, extending his hand warily. The northerner took it without hesitation and shook it emphatically. He smiled broadly and handsomely and replied: "I am Eldus Kabe. I am pleased to meet you Figs. Can I call you Figs?"

Eldus was an enigma to Figson. Passionate and outgoing, fiercely competitive, and oddly loyal, in spite of Figson never getting the sense of being completely trusted by him; it was hard for someone who had never been particularly social to get a grasp on exactly where he stood in Eldus's esteem. Was he his closest friend? It did not feel that way to Figson. But he never had a closest friend, so he couldn't know.

The stringy haired, olive skinned boy, with bony hands and baggy trousers always felt more an object of pity than a true friend. He could not understand why Eldus attached himself to him. But he could not deny that the positives of this acquaintance were immediate. His bullies were quickly tamed. In some cases, Eldus had charmed them enough for them to view the sidekick as an actual person, and because of Eldus, Figson had befriended a few, and managed some other respectful friendships at last. But Eldus always maintained the highest status, and Figson remained the shadow. But it was enough to make surviving law school possible, and at last, Figs could throw himself into his studies, and focus entirely on doing well.

He did not wholly let go of his interest in death arts during this time. He was welcomed into a small, secretive group he learned about through Eldus. He, Eldus and a few others with abilities for death arts pursued their interests together, experimenting in ways just edging on illegal, practicing the arts, and seeking out shadether pockets to see if they could have an effect on the dead. But Figson lost interest in the third year and dropped out of the club. The students and Eldus in particular were pushing the risks, and starting to toy with riskier things. Eldus was powerful, and Figson wasn't as committed. He instead put his energy into the schooling. He wanted to make his father proud.

Eldus immediately characterized Figson's abandonment of the club as his concession to Eldus being a better deathwitch. "It's all right, man, if you don't have it to compete with the rest of us. I understand," he said with an air of condescending largess. Figson let him think that, because he didn't really much care what Eldus thought on the matter. Instead he put away his books and papers on the subject for the time being. He wanted to do well in school, and make his father's and mother's investment in him pay off.

And he did. He graduated at the top of his class. He had always been at the top of the class. This was the only area in which Figson possessed the upper hand on Eldus; his scholarly achievements. Eldus had remained enormously competitive, and joked of his heartbreak every year Figson was awarded the honor of top student. Figson had come to recognize the glint of true resentment in Eldus' seemingly innocent remarks. He was not the type to glory in one-upping someone, like Eldus was, so he remained impassive, and continued to work hard. The golden northerner bore his personal humiliation mostly with forced grace, but he was not pleased to take second place to his shadow. Figson was furtively pleased by Eldus's remarks that exposed his disappointment about the matter. It felt like a victory; particularly when the young man spent so much time patronizing him over everything else.

After graduating, Eldus returned home to Dervra. Figson went back to Garvash. He was happy for his success, and also relieved that this phase of his life was over. He had enjoyed the learning, and he had achieved what he had started out to do. He had made his mother and father proud every year with a glowing record. Now, he wanted to move onto his new life. The work that was the relationship with Eldus was also something he did not regret leaving behind. Although grateful for Eldus' friendship, it was also wearing to be around someone who constantly compared, and competed, who was always judging, and never fully open. He wished Eldus well. It was time to go home.

He received, the moment he stepped through the door of his family home, a letter with the insignia of the most prestigious law firm on Garvash. "Ghellik and Yaymes," his father exclaimed as soon as he came to greet his parents in the humble drawing room. "Imagine that, Ghellik and bloody Yaymes!" He waved the letter about in pure joy. Figson could only smile, as his father was again so determined to put him on the right path, he forgot to even say hello.

"Hello father," Figson grinned and embraced the old man, taking the letter after he withdrew. He then turned to greet his mother, who was home specifically for his return, and who gazed benevolently upon them both. "Mother." He bent down to kiss her cheeks. She smiled at him.

"You are a bit of news about the place. Once the papers came from Trephyn with your graduation news and the placements, the buzz has been traveling about. The Tribune even published the scores of all the Garvashian students that did well; and you were right on top of the list. Over that Affenlock boy with all the money, even. Buzz buzz buzz! Top of the class. I never doubted you. Ask your father," she declared in her velvety loveliness. She was a beautiful creature at fifty; dark hair like silk plaited down her back, her well-tailored frock coat and breeches hugging close to her youthful curves. The feminine turn of her ankle and calf was only magnified by her top boots. He offered her a smile, and then sat down.

Figson finally looked down at the letter with a glow of pride and accomplishment. This was another victory. He tried to feel bad, but he could not; especially after he read the letter, with its invitation to join the ranks of the firm. Eldus had specifically mentioned this firm, when Figson had told him he was from Garvash. "That's where I plan to end up," Eldus replied. "I will hopefully be working at Ghellik and Yaymes. They recruit from the top graduates, so I am sure to be amongst the candidates. We can remain friends, then; for you will be nearby." As Eldus had said, only the top graduates with certain grade levels would receive the coveted offer. Eldus had expected it. Figson had never even dreamed. He had worked so very hard, he felt he deserved the honor, even if it meant his friend would be again disappointed, for he was not even among the top five. Figson put aside his thoughts of Eldus and instead focused on the letter. He would have to accept. There was no other option. Not with his father and mother so very proud, their tiny drawing room filled with their glee.

Figson rode into the city of Treelent the following morning wearing his finest suit of clothes, and met with Ardrich Yaymes, who looked as if he could have been Figson's relative. Also a gawky, awkward looking fellow, he immediately warmed to Figson, "Welcome to the firm, my boy," he was told by this venerable fellow over a vigorous hand shaking. "You will do great things, I foresee it. Come, let me introduce you to the partners."

Figson began his career with positivity. He established his place in the firm by securing the prosperous merchant Arrick Evlan within a month of his employment there. He also scored great acclaim for poaching Mr. Evlan from Knowells, Enk & Bane, the firm's direct competitor, and also the firm that now employed Eldus Kabe, attorney at law.

Figson carried a touch of shame at the idea that he might have fallen in love with a twelve year old girl. What he did not concede to himself was that in the beginning, it was the kind of love that was innocent and indulgent. It was a fascination with an exceptional creature, and appreciation of her unique and appealing nature. For it was impossible to be intelligent and insightful, and not immediately recognize the brilliant light in her eyes, and the sharpness of her gaze and not adore her for it. She dazzled him the moment he met her. And from that moment on, she had a special place in his heart that only grew and grew as the years passed.

It was a stiflingly hot day, and he had been invited to meet with Arrick. He did so quite often. With his international holdings and concerns, he required legal advice habitually. But for the past four years, it had always been conducted at his offices at Treelent. This time, Arrick was home with his family and didn't want to go into the city for the oppressive heat. The Evlan home was up the wooded hills by Highrocks Falls. The shade and cool breezes kept the tireless businessman at home. So Figson made the trip. He felt a special honor in being trusted enough to be invited into his best client's private home. He also looked forward to the cooler air.

He arrived in early afternoon and was immediately confronted by shouts of despair as Lady Naya Evlan stood over a long trail of watery footprints across the immaculate marble floor. "In the name of Ayonne, when I find out which one of you girls made this mess, I will sell you to gypsies!" She wailed, arms akimbo. She was a round, beautiful creature, with rosy cheeks and a plump, voluptuous shape. She had bright, searching eyes and a smirk edging on her full lips. She wore a white sheer day gown with a train that was sopping wet from being dragged through water. She noticed the young man in the open doorway and dropped her hands.

"Oh," she gasped, embarrassed. "You must be Figsy." She reached out her hand and sailed over to him. "You are welcome. I have heard so much about you, I think of you already as family. Come, let's get you to Arrick. I'll deal with the girls after. Dear Arrick is no great supporter of the summer heat. He threatens to take us north to Mahalav where his family is from. No thank you, I don't care for deep snow for months at a time, nor do I care for ghosts, and that isle is shot with shadether like nowhere else," she rambled, dragging a damp train along and collecting dust. She scuttled through a cavernous hall, across to a corridor, where various rooms passed by. She eventually found an innocuous door in a small connecting hallway, and shoved it open without leave, bursting into a comfortable office backed by six tall windows, all open to a courtyard with a vivacious fountain. Facing them was

Arrick with a pipe between his teeth and a stylus in his hand. He looked up from his writing.

"Good good. It's good you're here, I just found some documents you need for the acquisition of Kaydell Shipping. You ought to get your nose in them post haste so we can be prepared for the meeting tomorrow." No hellos, no goodbyes, lady Evlan was gone, and Mr. Evlan was throwing him into the thick of it. It was not unpleasant; there was a familiarity and warmth to being treated as such by this man and his wife. As if he belonged.

Arrick was a large, rather coarse man. He was peerage, but he had purchased his title and not inherited it. He was rich, imaginative and a skilled businessman. He was remarkably tall and broad. His physical appearance was typical of a Mahalavian, dark brown hair, shaggy sideburns, ruddy cheeks and a broad, welcoming smile. He had a pleasant, handsome face; what was once an exercise in handsome angles had been rounded out a bit from years of good food and little exercise. His eyes shone a delightful brown, and his teeth were as white as pearls, straight and attractive. Figson would soon see that all the Evlans were of excellent, healthy stock like the patriarch.

He sat at a large desk that was pushed up against a work table that was covered in a shuffle of documents. Beneath the table two grey, leggy, unkempt dogs were splayed out on the rug dead asleep, utterly disinterested in the newcomer.

The great windows were open, there was a comfortable breeze, and the fountain in the courtyard outside sang its freshness. "Take off that blasted frock, boy, you're making me perspire just looking at you." He obeyed and stripped off his coat. His thin linen waistcoat and cotton shirt helped cool him down quickly and wick away his perspiration. He sat down to look at the papers in question.

Mr. Evlan had been in high dudgeon most of the week because he was about to spend a sound sum on the purchase of a merchant shipping company. It was the one Figson's mother captained the Little Jezebel for. Arrick didn't trust the owner, and wanted Figson to make sure all the legalities were covered before they made the purchase. He picked up the stack of sheets; some inventorying the assets of the company, others outlining shipping routes and tossed them in front of Figson. He then flattened them under a thick ledger book charting out various years of finances. With a sigh, Figson dug in.

About a half hour later, a footman appeared with iced water. Evlan was one of the few men in the central isles who could afford a permafrost cellar filled with ice blocks stored from winter. It was like a gift from the gods on a day like this to wrap his hand around the cold, sweaty goblet and drain the frigid water from it. It chilled its way down his body and made him shiver. "I think you should adopt me sir, as your son, for I do very much want to live in a home with stored ice." Evlan laughed at the young man's assertion and gestured for the footman to refill the cups.

"If I can't be at Mahalav, I bring Mahalav to me," he replied. Figson laughed through his nose and kept working. It was a while later he noticed movement out in the courtyard. He leaned sideways for a better look and saw a slim girl with brownish blonde hair standing in the fountain. She had part of her skirt hems clutched in one hand, but the other hand was busy trying to keep hold of a wriggling stream otter. The rest of her skirts were sopping in water. The whole gown was soaked up to her knees. She wore stockings, which were visibly muddy and obviously sodden too. The front of her gown was brown with mud. She dropped the otter into the fountain and then knelt, , soaking the back of her skirts as she did. He then realized there were several more tiny otters paddling about in the water around her legs while she worked. She was submerging her arms up to her elbows, pushing something around under the surface. The fountain was so loud it absorbed all the additional splashing and sloshing made by this willowy child.

Figson observed this with interest, wondering what possibly would motivate a young lady to do what she was doing. Arrick glanced up at Figson when he fell still, and arched a brow when he saw his attention locked elsewhere. He followed Figson's line of sight, twisting in his chair. When he saw the girl he groaned in annoyance. "Oh, for death's sake, Dae what in the name of the gods are you up to?" The girl straightened and froze for a moment.

"The stream is dry. They were frantic," she blurted.

"Come here, but don't cross the threshold." Figson often thought back to this moment, and decided that it was the freckles to blame for his immediate affection for this young girl. There was such sweetness to the child. She lifted her thin little legs, wrapped in a trap of clinging cotton, one at a time, over the edge of the fountain, and waddled in a splashing mess across the cobbles to the window.

"Please explain why it was necessary to climb into the fountain? I now suspect I know why your mother has been shouting. If you insist on rescuing waterless otters, why not plop them in without ruining your frock and making rivers across the floor?"

"They needed their nest, father," she retorted. I had to place it at the right angle so it could still have access to air." Arrick pinched the bridge of his nose and took a long, measured breath.

"You carried their nest up here?" She nodded matter-of-factly.

"They have to have somewhere to rest or they'll drown," she added. "And they'll be more comfortable with something familiar in their new location. They drag the nests about themselves when they move; I had to do it for them, naturally."

Arrick took another deep breath and exhaled. He then picked up his pipe and chewed on it a few times. "Look here, little one... Get yourself upstairs and change into something dry at once. Take the servant's stairs and drop your over-dress at the laundry on your way. Don't let your mother see you in this state or the uproar will make any work around here impossible, understand?" She nodded and then knelt to grasp her sticky hems, careening off in a flurry of spattering footfalls.

Arrick then turned to Figson and grinned. "That was my eldest girl. The younger seems to have a little more sense about her. She's quiet and reads a great deal. Oh, but Dae she does come up with the most creative schemes. She makes me laugh. Naya is going to fly off the handle when she sees a family of otters in the fountain." He chuckled.

A while later, the door opened and a dry Dae appeared, smiling, carrying a plate of freshly chopped melon. She slid it onto the table where the two men worked. "Is this my reward for not turning you in for your ottery crime?" Arrick asked. She shook her head and kissed her father instead. She looked at all the papers and raised her brows.

"Can I help?"

"What do you think Figs, is there work for the girl?" Figson smiled at her earnest, unassuming face and nodded.

"Yes," he replied. "Sit here," he gestured to a free chair, "and see this stack of papers?" She nodded, sliding into the chair. "I want you scan each line, and take this quill and grey ink and mark the margin every time you see any of these company names mentioned," he handed her a small note page with several ports and shipping clients listed. "You think you can manage that?" She offered him a bold smile, twinkling at him, and emphatically nodded.

"Then get to work," he said with feigned sternness. She put her head down and began to read. He and Arrick had some melon, and then the three of them returned to silent focus, interrupted only by the occasional scratch of a quill and the splash of an otter.

Figson, having shown comfort and ease amongst the Evlan clan, was invited more and more often to join the patriarch in his office for work. His presence became so regular; the invitations began to extend to casual things, like a quiet dinner and evening walk with the family. Occasionally, he attended as a friendly guest at more formal events, like elegant evenings among their peers, at cards or dancing.

Mostly, he spent his time in Arrick's office, working quietly on the project of the time, sometimes with the assistance of Dae, who was keen to help anytime she could. Sometimes, Figson would be sent to work at the house alone without Arrick; so trusted he was by the family. It was then he and Dae formed their strange bond. He, the taciturn, sometimes stoic young attorney, she the growing, curious, bright young girl. It was a quiet, benign sort of relationship, almost of the brotherly sort.

One particular day, when Dae was fourteen, Figson took pause from his work to refresh himself, and left Dae to finish the ledger work she was completing for them. Arrick had also gone out to Treelent to see to some matters at the ware houses. When Figson pushed back his chair and exited, he knocked down the leather attaché which he toted wherever he went. It mostly contained some of his most current notes on matters, some documents that required signatures for his various clients and occasionally, some personal things he wanted to take with him throughout his busy day. He had been brushing up lately on his deathwitchery interests, and had crammed in there two volumes he wanted to read; one he had already read and wanted to reread, and a new book he'd found at a bookshop on his way up to Highrocks.

When the case fell over, the new book slid out on top of the shuffle of folded paper and vellum, the older book just beneath it. Dae reached down to tuck the things back into the case, and spotted the sharp gold lettering on the blue leather cover of the new book. Her interest was piqued. She plucked it from the pile, noting the other one beneath it. She took that one too. "A Comprehensive Study of Deathwitch Symbology," she muttered, her eyes reading the worn embossed script. She flipped open the well-worn cover of deep green leather. She opened the cover and saw Figson Howkes' name written in there in an elegant hand; with a year written in it. "To my dearest Figson. On the occasion of your Shertrath, I pass this on to you. Your mother," it said. The date marked was before Dae was born. *He must have owned this book at a young age*, she surmised. She knew what Shertrath was; it was the appearance of a Shadether Symbol on a young person. It meant someone was a deathwitch. The hair on the back of Dae's neck bristled. She put the old book back in his attaché, and reached for the newer one.

"Contemporary DeathWitchery and Death Arts – The Modernization of Ancient Applications Using Modern Chemistry," she read, turning the crisp, new book over in her hand. She cracked the cover, and leafed through the gold-edged pages, her brows arched in shock. The quiet man who indulged her so kindly—she never suspected he could be a deathwitch. She was still looking at the book when Figson returned. His brow furrowed at the sight of her wide, incredulous eyes when she looked up at him. He then saw the book in her hand.

"I cannot believe it is possible to accuse you of riffling through my attaché, Miss Dae, so I will conclude the book fell out," he sighed with an air of defeat.

"You knocked over your case when you pushed your chair back," she replied, relieved he wasn't angry. "I'm sorry, I didn't mean to pry, but I did not expect you to carry such a book with you."

"It's a gift," he lied. She raised her brow, and pursed her lip accusingly.

"That doesn't explain the one in there dedicated to you for your Shertrath," she added with classic teenaged sarcasm. Figson remained by the door and crossed his arms, tilting his head and suspiring yet again.

"I would very much like to say that it is none of your business, young lady," he said.

"I had no idea you were a deathwitch," she continued, a slightly awed smile curling on her lip. "What's it like?"

"It's like nothing," he dropped his arms and brusquely circled the table, snatching the book from her fingers and kneeling to sort out the disarray of the attaché case. "I don't practice. I practice law."

"But you still read about it," she added, gripping the sides of her chair and bunching up her shoulders in excitement.

"I am what I am, Miss Dae. I maintain an interest because it is in my blood; etched into my skin, and part of my life. I may not use the powers, but I should honor the gift by at least knowing as much about it as I can," he did not add that it was also a way of honoring his mother, and respecting her frustration for being prevented from practicing her gift.

"May I read the old book?"

"No."

"Oh, Mr. Howkes, please! I won't tell father, I promise." Even now, when the interaction was so comfortable between them, Figson could not be stern with her. And there was perhaps a guileless instinct in her head that her large eyes and freckled face had a powerful sway on the gawky lawyer. She did not have to beg further. He grumbled under his breath and fished in his case, removing the worn book.

"This is not just a book to me, it has greater meaning, which means: take good care of it, and I want it back in the same condition, nay, *better* condition in which you have received it," he said with false severity. She took it from his hand and smiled serenely at him. He looked at her as she opened the cover to browse it.

"I can't imagine you will find it very compelling or interesting," he said. She snorted through her nose and gave him a playful side-glance.

"We'll see. Perhaps I'll become a scholar of the death arts, you never know," she smirked.

"Oh, yes, your father would *love* that," he retorted. "Now, we promised your father we would have at least quarterly figures in order so he could work on that while we catch up with the Farreden accounts, so please put that somewhere safe and get back to the ledgers, or pass it to me," he said. Dae nodded, and slid the book into the side-pocket of her golden yellow day gown. She quietly went back to work. Figson sighed and resumed his position beside the table, scribbling away at her side.

Figson's place in the Evlan family only deepened. It was however, on the occasion of Dae's coming out ball, when she turned sixteen, that Figson realized he fostered deep feelings for his best client's daughter. At twenty seven years of age, going on twenty eight, he immediately felt like a shameless wolf.

Dae had asked him herself if he would attend the ball, and quietly whispered over some paperwork he and her father were studying, if Figson would start the first dance with her. "I would ask papa, but Miss Karring made a snide remark about how tasteless it was for girls coming out to start the dance with their fathers. I don't want to be called tasteless. Especially by a girl who wears a stuffed songbird on her bonnet," she grumbled.

"Perhaps you give too much importance to the opinions of girls who wear dead birds on their heads." He smiled warmly at her.

"I hate that I must, but I am surrounded by hordes of girls with dead birds on their heads. All are my peers and all are equally judgmental and bird-heady. I have enough trouble getting along with them. I hate them. But mother says that my acquaintance with them is important and I must value their ideas for they set the trends." She sighed heavily and furrowed her brow. "Mr. Figson. I already agreed with father that this was the best course of action, is that not true father?"

"Oh, yes. We did agree. And I am no great dancer. It's for the best." Mr. Evlan hardly glanced up from his ledger book.

"You know I would be deeply honored for the privilege of being your first dance partner for your special day, Miss Evlan. But I do hope you make the choice that will make you happy and not to please anyone else."

"Mr. Figson, I would dance with nobody other than you, if I could. You are part of our family. But mother insists that I dance each set with a new partner. So if I am forced to spend the evening dancing with strangers, I want at least one dance with someone I actually *like*."

"How can I say no then?"

"Oh good. What dance do you like best, so we can both look elegant and practiced?"

"I will learn whichever one you decide and practice with alacrity. I shall also go to the tailor and commission a fine blue coat for the occasion. I may not be handsome, Miss Evlan, but I can at least look noble and respectable." She frowned.

"Not handsome?" She studied his face for a moment. "Nonsense. In your fine blue coat, and your hair combed forward, you shall cut such a figure that all the dead-bird heads will be envious and wish you would dance with them." She then smiled in contentment and went back to copying figures from ledger pages. Figson stared a moment longer at her ink stained fingers and the tendrils of her hair slipping, as they invariably did, from her careful coif. He immediately was consumed with guilt.

They had spent the earlier part of the morning alone together, poring over a book of death arts, something that had become a bit of a habit between the two now that Dae was party to his secret. She had not found the subject itself very intriguing, but her fascination with Figson being a deathwitch did indeed catch her imagination. She sometimes found books on her own, and brought them to him when her father was out, to ask questions.

This book in particular described the various types of death-arts that existed; and the ancient types of power holders that no longer existed. Deathwitches were marginally common, not too difficult to find these days; but not quite as common as Ghosters, who were the most common death-power holders. Dae was intrigued by the extinct power holders.

"Why do they no longer exist?"

"I am not exactly sure. I believe because these kind do not inherit their power, they must be made," he said, looking at the beautiful hand-colored relief etchings of the different hierarchies of the ancient death-powers, starting with an image of a typical Ghoster in formal robes, revealing his markings, and rising up through the ranks into the extinct types, ending with a character called the Eminence; a willowy figure floating above the ground, hair splayed elegantly around his head; lifted by a swirl of spirits; surrounded by an aura of blood red.

"How can one make a power-bearer?" she asked.

"It doesn't say," he replied absentmindedly, leafing through the pages again.

"Why do these creatures no longer exist, Figson?" Dae asked, wide-eyed. He sighed and shook his head.

"They started disappearing centuries ago; just as deathwitches and ghosters seem to be doing nowadays. I suppose the shadethers are losing their ground in the living world, so there's no longer a great use for the creatures that bridge both worlds," he speculated. "As the ghosts linger, there is still use for ghosters, but death witchery has been made mostly illegal." Dae suspired.

"So someday, ghosts may no longer be part of our world?"

"It's possible," he replied. "I suspect this is a deliberate thing engineered by the systems of the living world. Our people have long wished to control and harness the shadethers, and I think perhaps the laws that forbid certain practices, and the society has grown to shun those that practice death arts, are part of a movement to make the shadethers disappear," Figson rambled absentmindedly. He then came back to himself, and suspired. "I venture that it is more than probable that making more of these shadether agents is a forbidden practice, or there would still be such Eminences and," he turned back the page a few times; "EtherGuardians."

"What do you suppose *they* did?" Dae asked, ogling the teal-aura and fearsome stance of the large figure with frightening runes etched into his face.

"I dunno; guarded the ethers?" he joked. Dae slapped his arm and giggled, and he felt the warmth of her nearness and he forced himself to sit back. They had been leaning closely together over the book, their cheeks only but a few inches apart. He ended the session quickly and directed her to either work or to make herself scarce. She chose to stay, and then later, her father returned and the question of the ball arose.

It hung heavily upon him, but he was almost willfully powerless against it. He entertained her desire for him to start the dance with him, and assured himself that he would do his best to look well for her, and to do her proud—even if he was fully aware that it only fed the inappropriate feelings he fostered for her.

Dae had learned a great deal about her father's business, about the legalities that accompanied his various dealings, and the structure of the complex concern that allowed them to live as peerage without inheriting the titles. Figson was always struck by how astute she could be, and quick to spot possible problems in the never ending shuffle of papers that crossed her father's desk. She would one moment be all wound up in things that young ladies were apt to think about, and the next act like a small version of her father, pointing out something or other that concerned her, that her father disregarded.

When Figson arrived on the evening of the ball, he was early; the first guest to come through the door. He was sitting on a bench in the great room, changing from his travel shoes to his formal slippers, when Dae sailed towards him in a draping of sapphire silk. He nearly fell off his bench at the sight of her. Unlike every girl he had ever known, she was already dressed and primped for the occasion; well before the guests began to arrive.

Her gown; the finest taffeta as light as air and shining like a jewel, swathed her slim form and trailed behind her. The hem, the narrow little bodice, the tiny puffed sleeves and the line down the front of her skirts sparkled with crystal beads and tiny pearls sewn on in delicate whorls. With this gown, she wore wheaten-gold gloves of kid leather wrapping her elegant arms. She had also petite gold slippers on her feet with sapphire beading sewn onto gold cockades on top of her shoes. Her usually difficult to manage, silken hair was tightly pulled against her head save for a set of perfectly buffed side-curls, and then arranged in an artfully woven bun behind a golden diadem with an arc of alternating blue paste gems and pearls. Delicate gold and sapphire jewelry adorned her swan neck and her gloved wrists. She also had lovely matching earrings dangling from her ears. Her sprinkling of girlish freckles seemed to transform from sweet to beautiful, and her large, searching eyes cut him cold. He sat in mid task, frozen by the beauty of this young woman.

"I am so glad you are here Mr. Howkes," she gasped in relief. "I wanted you to see something before this whole bother gets going," she rambled in her usual familiar tone. She took his arm when he stood, and glanced down at his feet; then at him. "You do look well, Mr. Howkes, if I may say so."

"You may, but only if you accept such a compliment in return, Miss Evlan. You are quite mind-bogglingly lovely, I must declare." She waved him off and dragged him towards the side of the house where the family spent their time. She led him to the offices and to some papers that were written in her delicate hand.

"It's the Kallenback concern. There were some irregularities in the docking fees at Cecilay. Father wasn't interested but I thought you ought to look. It's been on my mind all day."

Figson studied her figures and she was right. There were inconsistencies that only someone with a keen eye could see. What they could represent could not be determined until Figson could look into it in the next day or so. But he did not like the look of it, and neither did the observant Dae. He did not like Kallenback. He had the air of a swindler about him. He resolved to follow Dae's hunch. When he glanced back at her, he saw her expression was one of trepidation.

"Good eye, Miss Evlan," he said. Her breath exploded in relief.

"I knew I could count on you to listen. Thank you, Mr. Howkes. Perhaps I'm being suspicious over nothing, and allowing my personal feelings about Mr. Kallenback to skew my perspective on these numbers, but knowing you agree that they are not as they should be, well it makes me feel *so* much better," she gusted out.

"Yes. He *was* attentive to you the night before last, that Mr. Kallenback," he joked

"Oh, yeurgh, he's awful. He touched me without leave several times during the gaming. I made the excuse that Widow Baethen required my assistance and fled the table at once. I do wish mother and father were more attentive to these things," she lamented. "I received a gift from him today, a writing slope. I'd send it back, with regrets if I didn't love the thing so much," she snorted. Figson laughed.

"A gift is a gift; you could offend him by returning it."

"Yes. I'll take that," she replied. He smiled and offered her his arm.

"Come. I will pursue the matter of the figures, possibly as soon as on the morrow, gods willing. Let's blow out these candles and go back. You have guests to greet." She made a 'bleurgh' sound, snuffed the candles on the table, and clutched his arm; allowing him to escort her back to the part of the house that glistened in anticipation of the occasion.

When they returned to the hall, they were confronted by no other than the man in question. "I had no idea father invited him," she hissed under her breath. Mr. Kallenback was garbed in a rich suit of clothes that was a decade out of fashion. Overly ornate, and embellished in gold and silver embroidery, and beading more intricate than hers—it was a sight to see. It was a deep burgundy coat with a heavily pleated frock, a cutaway front revealing an unfashionably long waistcoat of striped tone on tone gold taffeta, and matching breeches of wine, with sag at the legs. He also wore a wig and side curls with a dusty queue. Arrick was speaking with him near the entrance from the foyer. When the older gentleman saw Dae, he stepped away from her father, and swept into a low bow, his eyes taking in the sapphire, befreckled jewel approaching him.

Figson looked quite plain in comparison to this dated fellow. A navy blue velvet coat with gold buttons, tan fall front breeches tightly fitted to his legs, a ruby waistcoat and white stockings with simple black court slippers. The high, layered collars and starched cravat gave him a sort of stiff, masculine elegance. He acknowledged the younger man with a bow and an overt sneer.

Figson had done as Dae recommended, and combed his lank, droopy hair forward as best he could. It stuck up wild in some places, but it looked quite fashionable. It was easy to overlook his severe features, rusty hair and plain face when he was starched up in finery.

"I do hope you will honor me with the first dance, Miss Evlan," the older man oozed. Dae blanched and then bit back her initial reaction. Figson could see her assume her poise.

"I'm afraid the first dance is already taken, Mr. Kallenback. I believe my card is full, for when I attended the promenade at the square with Miss Ailies last eve, she insisted upon introducing me to her acquaintances that were to attend tonight; and was quite strict about my accepting their bids for dances. The only person I know at all that I shall dance with tonight is our family's attorney Mr. Howkes. And I made him promise to dance the first with me last month!" She rambled like a giddy teenager, which was as affected and unlike her as he could imagine. He understood the depth of her capabilities then, and admired her intelligence.

"Had I known father had invited you, I might have thought to insist on one dance being left open, I am truly sorry sir," she continued. "There is always the chance one of Miss Ailies' beaus will decide not to come. I will surely let father know if that is the case." Mr. Kallenback frowned but bowed in assent, turning back to her father with a disagreeable expression on his face.

"Other guests are arriving, Dae. Go and greet them. And Figs, are those your riding boots?" Mr. Evlan pointed to Figson's old, worn top boots slumped by the bench where Dae had found him. With an uncomfortable smirk, he carried them to a servant to put away for the night.

As Mrs. Evlan was known for, the ball was a crush. The guests streamed in until Dae's poise began to fray, and she was so glad when Figson came to her rescue, and led her away towards the long room where the dancing would begin. The musicians and dance master were already making preparations, and the crowd of people strained at the doorway waiting for the guest of honor to make her way with her partner to the top of the room. Mrs. Evlan, in a gold gown with a fancy red turban topped with a tree of plumes, forged her way through the people to clear a path for her daughter.

The dance was announced by the master, who shouted: *Sweep of the Willow* and they took their places. As soon as they did, the remaining guests filed into the ranks below them, instinctively choosing their places based on their status. Figson had gone to a dance mistress for four weeks to learn the sets for this event. They were all new dances he did not know. He had practiced this one especially; almost obsessively. When the introductory notes were struck, he bowed to his partner, and she dipped down lithely into a curtsy, and the dance began. Several rows down, Mr. Kallenback danced with a spinster, but his face was invariably pointed up the set as the couple progressed towards them.

Figson chose to ignore the gasbag. He had for but this one dance, the loveliest partner he could hope for, who smiled at his smooth transitions of the dance, and showed pride that he had made the effort to learn it well. She did not converse with him. She merely gazed up at his face, hers aglow, her smile broadening when he setted like a true dancer, and turned her under to waltz her forward to the progression. They worked their way down the long line of dancers, managing to dance in a set with Kallenback without incident, and were perspiring by the time they were out for a round.

"Mercy, Mr. Howkes, you surprise me. I've never had more fun dancing before. You know it so well, I need not even think of what to do; you have it all in hand."

"You asked me to learn it, Miss Dae, so I did. I learned them all so I can ask other ladies to dance."

"I'm jealous. Nobody is dancing so well as you."

"Then I shall strive for mediocrity, and cast in the wrong direction at least once per dance if it pleases you." She giggled and they resumed dancing, now moving back up the set. The dance ended just before they were to encounter Kallenback again, and Dae grabbed Figson's arm before the man could assail her again, and pushed him towards a clutch of silk-clad girls. She allowed him to deposit her there.

"Thank you Mr. Howkes."

"I shall bring you some iced water," he said. He melted into the crowd and elbowed his way to the table where the faceted urns of sparkling cold water awaited. He filled two goblets and made his way back just In time to see Dae dragged off to the dance floor again by a young man closer to her age. She was smiling and chatting away at the rosy-cheeked fellow. He felt stupid all of a sudden.

He turned to the spot where the girls had been, and found their numbers depleted. He saw a girl of less advantageous means lingering near two others. He offered the two finer ladies the water, which was graciously accepted, and then put out his hand to the girl in the plain muslin dress trimmed haphazardly with ribbons and shabby little silk flowers that looked like they'd been plucked from a bonnet. She was pretty in a conventional way, and made timid by the splendor that cast her into the shadows. Shadows, he understood. Shadows, he could relate to.

She colored at the attention but accepted his hand, and he led her to the bottom of the set. He felt like Kallenback, glimpsing upwards in some desperate desire to catch a flash of sapphire as he danced this long progression with his frightened partner. The evening progressed and he saw Dae only from afar, surrounded by beautiful, rich young people. His heart hurt at the idea that he simply was not good enough for Dae.

****

"Mr. Howkes, I am surprised at you. You seemed so content to focus on the Evlan account. There is enough there to keep you occupied and your contributions to the firm are undoubtedly sufficient," Mr. Yaymes blurted after a significant period of silent introspection over Figson's request. Figson was startled by the sudden exclamation.

"I don't know how to say this without sounding half mad, but I have a desire to improve myself Mr. Yaymes. To make myself worthier. I am no dandy, and I have middling looks at best. I must compensate sir, by becoming of financial consequence."

"I see. So this has to do with a lady," Yaymes concluded.

"Yes. She is well above me, and too good for me. So I must make myself worthy. And quickly," he added, "before she gets snapped up."

"Indeed," Yaymes muttered. He sat down and tamped out a pipe. He stuffed it from a leather tobacco pouch, his eyes fast on the worn top of his desk. "Hmm, hmmm," he grunted. He picked up a lighting wick and jabbed it in the candle flame, still ruminating.

"Listen… Go and bag another big client. If you can do that, and relinquish him to a partner as you should focus on Evlan, I will speak to the Mr. Ghelliks both, and see if we can use that strategy to supplement your current income. If you can do it once, then I can convince them you can do it again. Catching the big fish is the most laudable and precious thing an attorney can do in this firm. Any one of our associates can handle the legalities; it's the acquisition that's the challenge. If you do that, even once, your standing in this firm improves. You are engaging and competent, clever and bright. Use those skills to catch the big ones, Mr. Howkes. You do that enough, and there will be no lady in this city good enough for *you*."

Figson returned to the Evlan home a week after the ball to sit down with Arrick to discuss his findings on Dae's request. Arrick was agitated already as his younger daughter Renna had fallen from her pony and hurt her ankle, and Dae was extremely angry with her Father about something or other and was ostensibly locked in her room, although Figson had seen her at a distance at the falls, rolling big rocks over the edge into the lake.

"He is doing what?" he barked.

"Padding his expenses for bribes sir," Figson replied evenly. "Turns out only three of the import permits are legitimate. They are only so because they were acquired through his purchase of the Higsom routes. The remaining nine were denied for reasons currently unknown. He has been bribing the port masters in several ports of Cecilay, and doing business without the proper permits. Your daughter was the one that caught it," he added. Arrick growled under his breath.

"He asked me permission to propose to Dae yesterday. I could not tell him no. He is a valuable asset to the shipping division of my company. I don't like it. But I felt obligated to allow him to ask." He paused. "Now that he is shown to be dishonorable, can I not tell him I've changed my mind?"

"Not until I get more details from the Cecilay port authority. I need firm evidence before you confront him with anything."

"Oh, and Dae is raving mad at me. Steaming," he added.

"He *is* a bit long-in-the-tooth," Figson ventured boldly, knowing full well that he too was long-in-the-tooth; perhaps not quite so as Mr. Kallenback, but too old nonetheless. Arrick merely nodded.

"She is such a singular girl. I never know what will please her on that end. He is sickeningly rich. More than I am. She would want for nothing."

"Except love, and happiness," Figson grunted. Arrick threw himself back into his chair.

"I never have been able to grasp how so many of my peers can treat their children like consideration in a contract. I failed Dae."

"She won't accept him, you needn't fear," Figson concluded with confidence, seeking to give him peace.

"I hope not. I shall stress that her happiness is paramount. I shall refrain from overtly influencing her, but criminal or not, I gave him my blessing to ask. How obtuse I can be sometimes," Mr. Evlan murmured. "I fear that she might accept in fear of jeopardizing our investments with Kallenback. She has come to understand the business well, and to take a sense of ownership to her part in it."

"Give her leave to decline, and she will." Arrick nodded.

"Yes. He will be here soon. Your presence will embolden her. That I know. You are her ally. Stay for dinner." Figson was surprised by this assertion. He felt the swell of warmth that filled his chest and he lowered his face to hide the pleasure it gave him.

Kallenback was visibly angry at the sight of the attorney. "I saw how she smiled at him, he is an interloper and a fortune hunter, mark my words," he heard the man hiss to Arrick. Figson had to give his client credit for his poise and calm.

"Be so kind as to go and find the infernal child, Figson if you would," he pleaded. Figson nodded and set off to the falls. He encountered Dae in the orchard, dawdling on her way back to the house.

"That odious fetid old gasbag is there isn't he?" She snarled. Figson nodded. She glowered balefully and he saw her eyes moisten.

"You are well within your rights to say no."

"Father wants me to marry him! What would that... that... Heap of dung be capable of if I decline? He could try to ruin father!" Her agitation was increasing and a plump, shining tear plopped onto her freckled cheek and rolled down, dripping onto the bodice of her muslin gown.

"Nonsense. He no more wants you to marry him than you do. He is in no position to tell him he can't propose. But he will rejoice if you defy him." She sniffed and wiped the wetness from her eyes with the ball of her fist. Figson fished in his pocket and handed her a tattered, worn kerchief. She took it and swabbed her eyes clean.

"I know he's up to no good," she said.

"He is. I just need Cecilay to send me the evidence that will allow your father to dissolve the connection and protect his holdings." Hope filled her eyes and she smiled through her despair.

"Then take me home, Mr. Howkes."

The scene that ensued was a grim one. Clutching against his chest was his beloved Dae, trembling like a leaf, her face pressed into the crook of his arm, weeping. Arrick, his nose bloodied and fists bruised was hunched in a chair by the window, watching the militiamen brusquely load Kallenback into the coach he came in, but with his hands tied, and a flanking of menacing guards to surround him. When Figson pushed Dae back to see her face, he had to fight his own urge to set that coach ablaze with Kallenback in it. She had a colossal bruise forming across her cheekbone, and her eye socket was swelling and turning a terrible shade of purple.

"I'll take her to her room, I hope you will overlook the impropriety considering the circumstances," Figson said. Arrick raised his hand and shooed them. He huddled her close to him and stooped to catch her behind her knees with his other arm, lifting her slight frame up and carrying the weeping girl to her apartments.

The house was still. Mrs. Evlan and Renna had gone to visit friends, deliberately sent away for the proposal. The servants were nowhere to be seen, likely below floors getting the story from the man servants that had wrestled Kallenback to the floor and escorted him out to greet the militia.

He found Dae's abigail in her rooms putting away a basket full of folds of fresh, snow white linens. She leapt into action, peeling back the coverlet of her bed. She pulled off her slippers before Figson could lay her gently down.

"I am sorry this happened, Dae."

She sniffed and scooted back onto her pillows, putting one in front of her chest and clutching it. She sighed. "I'm not," she said defiantly. "This moment only guaranteed that he will never show his face here again, regardless of what we discovered about him. It was worth it. It has also made me resolve to marry someone I want. I will no more accept these strategic proposals, even if it threatens to crumble my father's empire."

"Good girl," Figson smiled. She brushed her fingers over her wounds and winced. Figson's smile formed into a thoughtful frown.

"I ought to go. It isn't seemly for me to be here."

"You are so good, Mr. Howkes." He shook his head and strode out, leaving Dae in the hands of her abigail. He decided it was time to go for the day. He had to secure a new client for the firm. He had more time now, thanks to Kallenback. The odds that Dae would be swept off her feet anytime soon were reduced to nothing with one botched proposal from a crooked businessman.

Determination had always been the one thing Figson could count on in himself. And determination won him a higher status at Ghellik and Yaymes, and he had earned himself the distinction of a nickname from the partners. The Foxhound.

Figson had bolstered his flagging confidence with the affection he felt for Dae, and used that to turn himself into a fully fledged salesman. He researched his quarry, found what he needed to show his value and that of his firm, and return to the partners with a contract clutched in his hand. He became proficient at the social aspect of business, and almost always got his man, or in two cases so far, his Zillig woman.

In eight months, he brought the firm nine new clients; people of means and influence. His main client remained Mr. Evlan, but he also now had Mrs. Thyne, and the infamous actor and performer, Darvus Rann. The other acquisitions were passed onto junior partners and rising associates.

He spent more time away from the Evlans now, attending to his new clients, entertaining prospective ones; attending events and conducting business. As Arrick walked in the higher circles of the Garvash society, he encountered him more often than not when he engaged in his work, and Arrick expressed with sincerity that his presence was more than once missed by all at home.

The time he did spend with Arrick was more business related now, as he had less time to divide with the family. Upon Dae's insistence, business was conducted as much as possible from home, so she could work with them as they always had.

Arrick had an idea why Figson suddenly threw himself into his work with such intensity. He was beginning to see the burgeoning regard in his daughter as well. She had always liked the young man, but since the ball of her coming out, her entire manner changed when it came to the subject of the family attorney. She seemed more respectful of him, and she valued his time with the family more. He knew the boy was working to make himself financially equal to her peers, so he could be amongst the few who would be of suitable status to take her as a bride.

Arrick had no objections, and admired Figson's resolve. He saw him rising up through the ranks of his colleagues and peers. He overheard Bael Ghellik dropping the word partner when Figson's name came up, more than once at the club. And the club to which these affluent gentlemen belonged was also eyeing the young fellow as a possible new inductee. Figson was doing all the right things to earn his right to ask for Dae's hand. Arrick supported it wholeheartedly. He liked the young man.

During this period, the firm of Knowells, Enk & Bane took it upon themselves to begin soliciting more aggressively for clients as well. Someone at the firm got wind of Figson's grand efforts, and fearful of having more valuable clientele poached by the Ghellik and Yaymes' Foxhound, they sent out their own agents to compete for, and defend any prospects from their competitors. To be expected, the man leading this initiative was Eldus Kabe. Figson first encountered him at the opera one evening, as he accompanied a party of well-to-do fellows and a few ladies. It was the first time he had seen Eldus since they parted at graduation. There was a formal, somewhat terse greeting exchanged, and that was all. But as the months rolled by, Eldus became a common sight at society events. Eldus came from affluence. He was natural to it. He fit right in, as he had when he arrived at university. Figson held his ground, but Eldus was at his heels, nipping. Never once had he had the advantage as of yet. But inevitably, the time came when Figson's world became threatened by Eldus' influence. And that was when Eldus set his sights on Dae.

It began at the annual cotillion ball at Clareth, an event to which only the most affluent were invited. Figson, having just been inducted into the gentlemen's club, and having just purchased a fine town house of his own, was among the elite to be invited. He had been asked by Arrick to accompany Dae as her escort for the event, and he was delighted to consent. He met them at their home and rode in the coach to Clareth. Dae, once again, was a vision. This time in a regal looking gown of slate grey, decorated in brassy accents. She looked grown up at eighteen. The two years of reflection and calm after the ball had made her slightly too serious for the taste of her mother and father. Figson found her elegant and poised. He had taken care to choose only the best clothing for himself, enough to look fitting with Dae, but not so much to outshine her.

She discussed legal matters mostly in the coach, sitting beside her mother and sister. But Figson was conscious of her foot pressed against his; so much so, he could feel the warmth of her body emanating into his through their shoes. He sat across from her and gazed through the meager light, to catch a glimpse of her graceful neckline, and her sweet freckles. He was thinking that perhaps it was almost time to ask Arrick the big question. Tonight would be the answer.

They arrived with the throngs, their coach merging with the slow line of arrivals, the noise of the guests seeping into the carriage.

Torches shed golden flickering light into the space, and the sound of music could be heard, growing clearer with each beat of the hoof. They were soon stopped at the stairs of Clareth house, and the gentlemen disembarked first in order to hand the ladies out. Figson, proud and adoring of his prize, handed her down as if he was showing her off to the world.

They entered the house, handed their cards to the caller, and waited. "Mr. and Mrs. Evlan, Miss Dae Evlan, Renna Evlan and Mr. Figson Howkes," the wigged man belted out over the din. Faces turned in recognition, some hands went up to wave in greeting, and the family party descended into the hall, melting into the glistening crowd.

Dae clung tightly to Figson's arm. She had declared to him after her coming out that she did not like such gatherings. "I will only dance if it is with you," she told him as they diverged from the family party, and forged through the crowd. "Do not leave me alone again," she warned him. "I don't want to be swept away,"

Figson arched a brow. "Again?" She stopped him and gazed up at his face.

"As you did at my coming out," she replied with a touch of hurt. He was taken aback.

"What could you possibly mean?"

"After the first dance, you abandoned me to the throngs. I didn't see you at all the whole night after that."

"I beg your pardon Miss Dae, but I never abandoned you. I went to fetch water and when I returned some young fellow had caught your arm and taken you away. You clearly said your dance card was full, and you had partners for every dance. Was I ill informed?"

"You should have come back for me," she muttered with a frown.

"You hold this against me after two years, and mention it to me now?" he asked laughingly. Dae knew she sounded absurd, but the first time at a large gathering since her own, had brought back a rush of feelings unexpectedly. She squeezed his arm and shook her head.

"Stay with me, if you would."

"I am your escort this time, Miss Dae. I've no intention of relinquishing you to *any* ruddy-faced high brow buffoon that comes along." She smiled.

"I feel much better then," she declared. He led them forward to an area where a group of young men and women were gathered. The men and one woman were colleagues at the firm, and the additional people were their guests and acquaintances.

"Ah, Figsy, glad you're here. Gale here says he might have a tip for a prospect for you," a dark haired young man declared at the sight of Figson.

"You can discuss that later. No lawyer-babble tonight, you promised!" a mousy little lady in a buttercup yellow gown barked. The clutch of attorneys chuckled and relented, making introductions instead. Figson introduced Dae. Since her ball, and the Kallenback incident, Dae had withdrawn significantly from her already infrequent social activities. She remained home, rode her horse, took walks and worked with her father in his office when she could. This was the first ball she had attended since. She hardly knew anyone of note anymore, and hardly anyone knew her.

"I'm for a dance," someone muttered. "Shall we herd over there and elbow our way into some sets?" It was agreed, and the group made their way to the hall where the cotillion dances were underway.

"I haven't practiced like I should," Dae murmured to Figson. He glanced down at her worried face.

"Do you want to just sit?"

"No, let's do this one dance to start. You know it?"

"Sadly, yes. Too well. I've been forced to practice these with Lady Ackswor's daughter."

"Why?"

"Prospective client." She frowned at this.

"Does she expect you to court her daughter too?"

"No. Filanema is impossibly timid. I offered to help ease her worries about attending this event. And she is there, ready to dance," he pointed subtly to the girl. She had a long face, and long teeth that didn't fit in her mouth. She was dancing with a young man equally as gawky and uncertain. They both looked at ease, smiling at one another as the cotillion sets formed. Dae and Figson joined their set. The young woman beamed at Figson when she saw him, and gave Dae a warm smile. Another couple joined their set, and then a fourth. To Figson's annoyance, it was Eldus, dancing with the daughter of another of his recently acquired clients. He gave Figson a stiff bow in greeting and then looked at the woman clutching Figson's arm with mild interest. The music soon began after that. And Eldus watched with growing curiosity, the twinkling smiles Dae cast onto Figson. At the end of the dance, when they honored their partners, Eldus bowed to Figson, and when he looked up, he glanced at Dae's glowing cheeks and possessive grip on Figson's arm, and a strange, cruel little smirk twisted on his handsome lips.

It wasn't Figson's place to tell Arrick who he should or should not befriend. He was not concerned that he would lose Mr. Evlan as a client, but he was alarmed to find Eldus had insinuated himself into the circle in which he and Arrick partook. Unlike Figson, Eldus had a pedigree. He was accomplished and well-spoken, charismatic and charming. He was also extremely handsome and rakish. Mrs. Evlan immediately adored him, and it made Figson realize how benign her affection was for him; she liked him like a member of the family. But by her behavior around Eldus, it became clear that Naya did not count Figson as a worthy suitor for Dae. She remained selectively blind to Dae's increasing attachment to Figson.

Eldus was frequenting more events, and making himself known to the Evlans. Dae's anti-social nature was the only saving grace at this point, for she did not go out often; and it denied Eldus access to what was now most markedly his target. But there was no lack of trying on his part, and Figson was growing increasingly concerned.

He found Eldus hanging about the Club one afternoon. He was Arrick's guest. And he was busily ingratiating himself to other members when Figson entered the room. He paused in the doorway when he saw Eldus seated by the bay window with a couple of gentlemen, amiably chatting. Figson frowned, turning to the breakfront to serve himself a stiff drink

"Ah, it's Figs! Who let *him* in here? I thought they were selective about who they allow through these doors," Eldus laughed when he saw the slim, red-haired figure sliding through the cavernous sitting room towards the breakfront. "Come sit with us, scarecrow. We were just talking about you. I was telling them about the first time I met you," he said with a mocking smile. The gentlemen did not look as amused or impressed as Eldus was with himself. Figson drained the snifter of the viscous pear brandy, and sloshed a few more ounces into the empty glass before making his way to where he sat.

Arrick entered the room and walked over as well, filling his pipe from his waistcoat pocket, and used a candle to suck the flame into the little bowl. Eldus repeated the tale of the day he met Figson. Arrick's brow furrowed and he drew on his pipe a few times, puffing out blue clouds of fragrant smoke. He then lowered it when Eldus laughingly said, "If it weren't for me, where would our little scarecrow be today? Eh? You should thank me, Figs."

"Seems like he's been doing quite well without your protection, these days, don't you think? Youngest candidate for partner in the history of Ghellik and Yaymes, an unimpeachable reputation of honor and integrity in his circle, and one of my most trusted friends. Seems a little low to try to embarrass the boy for being bullied by a pack of gibbering idiots back at university, don't you think?" Figson's heart swelled at Arrick's words. The older man seemed irritated with himself. Eldus waved it all off as a joke, and continued babbling on about his new curricle and hack. Arrick patted Figson's shoulder and gestured with a nod of the head for him to sit elsewhere with him. They chose a corner of the room away from the laughter and Eldus's noise, and sat down in deep leather chairs—the autumn air seeped into the austere old townhouse that housed the club, and they chose to sit close to the fire.

"I don't often bring guests to the club. This is the first time I've actually regretted it. I won't repeat *that* mistake."

"Eldus is Eldus," Figson murmured, putting the snifter to his lips, his eyes lost in a faraway place momentarily. "Who am I to say he doesn't belong here? He is a blue-blood after all. He can afford to walk in this circle and pay the club dues." Arrick harrumphed at that, and drew from his pipe, gusting veils of smoke between them.

"But you don't like him?"

"I honestly cannot say I ever did, Arrick. He was kind initially. He was ostensibly my friend, but he was keener on making everyone see how big of a person he was to befriend a little squirrel like myself than he was actually being a friend. I always felt that I was about appearances. It's always been about appearances."

"Hmm, yes," Arrick replied thoughtfully. The two sat in quiet contemplation. "If he were to be inducted, it would surely be uncomfortable for you."

"My feelings are irrelevant, as I'm a junior member and do not have a vote."

"That answers my question," Arrick chuckled. Figson smiled.

"Naya seems to like him a great deal. She's invited him to join us for dinner tomorrow evening. He will stay for cards. I think you should come too," Arrick said. Figson smiled.

"As long as Naya welcomes me."

"Why would she not?" Arrick looked at Figson, and the younger man sighed, his expression so meaningful and telling, that Arrick realized what the young man was thinking.

"I see. Well, I invited you. So be there," he blurted decisively. "That's that." Figson nodded in assent and took another drink.

"Then I shall be there with my bag of fish."

"Bag of fish?" Eldus's voice interrupted them as he walked just into earshot as Figson spoke. "Going carding?"

"Tomorrow evening," Figson replied levelly. "Arrick has invited me to dinner and cards. I was telling him that I planned to bring my little bone fish." Eldus's face soured a bit, but he recovered quickly.

"You will gamble with *fish*? Not very sporting," Eldus barked out in laughter.

"I do not allow gambling with money under my roof, Mr. Kabe," Mr. Evlan interjected. The northerner raised his brows, and was for a moment without anything to say.

"I suppose I could bring some of my own chits," Eldus said, sitting near them.

"Excellent," Arrick replied with a bored sigh. Figson drained his glass, and crossed his legs, staring at the fire.

"I am looking forward to tomorrow evening, Mr. Evlan," Eldus said with a large smile. "I find the company of your family most gratifying." He said this with measured words, his eyes on Figson, who remained impassive. Arrick was getting the sense of the spite that was being bandied about by this stranger, Figson recognized his silent acknowledgement of it. The way he tended to gnaw on his pipe and dig his chin into his cravat when he was irritated.

"Your daughters are also most pleasant company as well, sir. Most pleasant. Bright creatures, with excellent conversation. Especially the eldest, Miss Dae. She is a rare gem, sir. Accomplished and lovely. Superior to all the ladies I've had the pleasure of meeting of late," he gushed. Figson could scarce keep his temper.

"My daughters are anything but conventional, Mr. Kabe. They are unique. They do not have a great deal in common with their peers. They are intelligent and astute. They see the world for what it is." Eldus paused and looked at Arrick with an expression of puzzlement. Arrick, thoroughly disgusted at last, grunted as he lifted himself from the deep chair, and shuffled out of the room without a word.

"What do you suppose that was about?" he asked Figson. The young man looked at Eldus with an arched brow and pursed his lips.

"He's saying that Dae cannot be won like other girls; with flattery and romantic attention. She is a unique creature. An incisive and wise creature. She may seem to be as hapless and silly as her friends, but she is far from it. She sees people for who they are, Eldus."

"What do you imply with that, Figs?" Eldus became serious.

"Take from it what you will, Eldus. Arrick merely says that his daughters might not be to your taste. They are more complex than their peers." Figson stood and put his dirty glass on the tray by the clean ones, and looked back at Eldus as he exited the sitting room. The golden haired rake was glaring daggers at him.

"Figson!" Eldus called out. "I would not discount my abilities with the ladies, if I were you," he said provocatively. Figson stood in the doorway, staring at his old friend, whose air radiated malevolence like Figson had never seen before.

"I'll trust Dae to decide what's best for her," Figson replied. The golden-haired man laughed darkly and turned away, a baleful smile across his mouth. Figson furrowed his brow, and wondered what the man could possibly be thinking. He left him in the sitting room, opting to return to Highrocks early to spend a few hours with the family before the guests arrived for dinner.

Eldus flirted relentlessly with Naya, who soaked it up with alacrity. He sat near her for dinner, and his low voice could be heard, followed by Naya's ebullient laughter. "Oh, Mr. Kabe, you are a brute. Dae, you would be so shocked by the things this man says," she declared. Arrick and Figson darkened at Naya's impropriety, and her affection for this northern cad.

After dinner, when the small party was settled at the tables for cards, Naya insisted that Dae take Eldus as a gaming partner. Figson played with the widow Thacken, and watched from afar as Eldus worked his wiles on Dae, who remained kind, polite and talkative, but quite impassive and unresponsive to his overt flirtations. Renna then asked Figson to partner with her, and he spent most of the evening working to help Renna win as many fish as possible, for Mrs. Evlan had obtained a prize for the person who won the most fish in the first round of cards; a beautiful writing slope made of stunningly grained silkwood, inlaid with ebony and mother of pearl. Renna wanted it dearly. "It's nicer than Dae's," she declared.

Renna had always been a quiet little figure, often avoiding notice. As she grew older, she remained introverted. She crafted and read frequently, and spent a lot of time with Dae. They were close, and they grew closer the older they became. Renna had always accepted Figson for face value and treated him like an elder brother. Dae and Arrick liked him a great deal, and that was all she needed to be convinced of his value to the family. She did not go out of her way to spend time with him to the degree that Dae did, but she could rely on his friendly interaction and support, like a kindly big brother. He did not fail her this time either, and he supplied her with the fish she needed to claim the beautiful prize. In celebration, she sat at her harp and sang a beautiful song for the company before the second round of gaming began. The group then threw themselves into the kind of games that did not require fish.

Eldus' attentions migrated from mother to daughter, until he monopolized Dae for the rest of the evening, occasionally catching Figson's eye to offer him a smug little wink or grin. It didn't bother Figson as much as Eldus hoped; at least not in any outward way. He paid his attention instead to Renna, helping her find all the secret compartments in her new slope, and sitting with her to sort out and separate the pile of fish so they could be returned to their rightful owners. He and the younger sister chose to recuse themselves from the gaming this round.

During the course of the evening, something strange began to happen. Dae, oddly, seemed to become increasingly interested in Eldus. Her normally calm and poised air became animated and even flirtatious. She started acting like a typical young woman, the kind that flushed and giggled at the attentions of a gentleman.

He watched this with incredulity. He noticed Arrick also watching with a puzzled brow. Renna was forthright about the strangeness of it all. "Good gods, did Dae tipple too much? She is carrying on like a half wit," she snorted with her lip twisted in distaste.

"Indeed," Figson muttered in astonishment. He forced himself to look away, and engaged Renna in a puzzle at the round table instead, far away enough from the shameless exhibition his dearest Dae was becoming. He was concentrating on that when there was a commotion, and he turned around in his chair. He witnessed Naya embracing Dae, and the saw the look of abject horror on Arrick's face. He then heard above the voices of the other guests, Naya's excited cry:

"Oh joy! To be married!"

"Just a moment!" Arrick shouted. "I gave no permission for a proposal!"

"Father, please!" cried Dae in a most uncharacteristic way.

"Absolutely not! I forbid it!" Dae threw her hands to her mouth and sobbed loudly, suddenly dashing from the room and into the darkened hall. Naya also began to weep, and admonished her husband as a cruel tyrant, and she too stormed away. The guests, uncomfortable and discomfited, began to rise and make their excuses to Arrick. Eldus sat where he was, arms crossed, glaring at Arrick.

"Get out of my house," he snarled at Eldus.

"She agreed to marry me, it is what she desires. You've no right to interfere." He stood and stalked towards the door. "I'll be back for Dae." Figson and Renna remained still, and Arrick did not move until the last person was gone. He then turned to Figson.

"What just happened?" He asked, edging on a rage.

"Your guess is as good as mine," Figson retorted. "Who was that girl? It certainly wasn't Dae. One night of whispers and flirtation so wholly out of character, and she becomes engaged; over cards?" He shook his head. "I feel like I'm standing outside of my body and seeing this as a stage performance."

"I want to know what he did," Arrick growled.

Renna stood and patted down her skirts. She looked first to her father and then to Figson. "If I'm not mistaken, Dae was acting as if she was possessed. The whole thing reminded me of the book Trapped by Deception." They gazed at her questioningly. She sighed heavily and impatiently at their ignorance and crossed her arms. "The villain of the story is a deathwitch. He captured a specter of a dead woman, and threatened to destroy her if she didn't do as he said. So using this poor spirit, he forced a possession. The heroine became someone else, just long enough to walk into her bank and to withdraw her fortune, which she bestowed upon the villain, before the ghost was freed. The heroine awoke destitute, and the story goes on to tell how she had to fight to regain her status and capture the villain."

"Dearest Renna," Figson whispered. She shook her head at her father's silence and bade them goodnight. "I'm going to go find Dae," she declared. In a bustle of silk, she trotted out to the rooms she shared with Dae. Arrick moved to Figson, his face still expressing his horror.

"What are you thinking Fig?"

"That Renna and her constant reading, is a perfect godsend."

"Only a deathwitch or a ghoster could do what she described," Arrick opined. Figson nodded. He felt so separated from that world these days. Garvash was so quiet on the spectral scale, and he hadn't thought about the arts for years. To hear of these things were shocking, and jarring. It drew him back to the days at university, sitting around a table in the medical wing during the evenings, experimenting with powders and elements. He looked at Arrick with a slightly guilty expression.

"Eldus *is* a deathwitch. And I confess that I am one as well. But I have not practiced any arts in years. Neither of us was formally educated in these things, but we have both the powers and dabbled in the arts at university. In secret. I have never heard of a forced possession, but I wasn't there for the duration with the death arts club. I had no idea a deathwitch could do such a thing. I imagine it must be like pulling a spirit from the ether to animate a newly formed body, except doing it with a living body. But how, I do not know. I dropped out of the club to focus on my studies. I wonder if we can prove this. Is Dae still influenced by this ghost?" He shook his head in confusion, and frowned darkly. "I must apologize Mr. Evlan, but I must go," he said. Arrick put his hand on Figson's shoulder.

"She agreed to marriage in front of witnesses. He can make his claim even if Dae recalls nothing of it. He can claim a great sum for the breaking of his verbal contract with Dae," Arrick did not need to remind Figson of the rules of engagement. He merely nodded in acknowledgement of Arrick's concerns and then rushed out.

Figson discovered a plethora of compelling information when he received the messages in reply to his own. He stood in the rookery at Ackham for the fourth day in a row, where three of the four responses he was expecting from Dervra and Trephyn arrived on the talons of heela kestrels. When the fourth finally arrived in a whistle of feathers, he set out back to Highrock Falls to speak to Arrick. He found Dae, stricken and shocked in her father's office, her eyes puffy with tears. He needed no explanation from her. And his look assured her of such. She sniffed, and rubbed her eyes with the heel of her hand. Her father looked at him with a pointed, urgent glare. Renna was present as well, for the first time he could ever recall, sitting in the office with her sister.

"The man we see in Eldus is only a partly finished portrait. I have discovered so much more. I have messages from his father, from classmates and from a friend experienced in deathwitchery," he declared decisively. He sat down at his usual spot at the work table and sighed heavily. "Eldus was disinherited. He has been for years. When he arrived at university he had just been cast off. So he left Dervra and came to Trephyn. He misrepresented his financial means to his firm as well. Where he has been getting the funds he has beyond his wages is a mystery. I wager if we look into it; he probably has an army of creditors after him. But it is clear he has an eye on Dae's fortune to save him," he rambled. "He dabbled in possessions with the deathwitch club. They all did. And as Renna so astutely pointed out the night of the dinner, he forced a specter into Dae and made her promise to marry him in front of twenty people. In front of me," he added, looking at Arrick with wide eyes. Dae gazed back as well, stricken and silent, her face pale.

"We have enough, do we not, to undermine the validity of the proposal?"

"Yes," Figson assured him, handing him letters. "Cost me a month's wages in hawks but it was entirely worth it."

"That is a crime. What he did is a crime," Renna spoke. Figson nodded.

"A ghoster can validate that she was possessed."

"We will summon one at once. With these other letters, we can prove his motive." Arrick grinned and snatched the letters from Figson. "Summon lieutenant Drathe from the militia, Figs. I want that scoundrel caught."

The judge was quick to issue a warrant based on the information that was given to him. The confirmation from the ghoster only added to the immediacy of his capture. A search was ordered, and the militia sent to Eldus' residence to arrest him came up empty handed. Vital items were missing including the new curricle and horse. How he got wind of their having discovered his plan, there was no way to tell. The quarry had already fled. He had plenty of time after the dinner to escape while the Evlans and Figson scrambled to suss out what had happened.

The scandal was immediate as well. It spread through the town like wildfire, and as to be expected whenever the death-powers, or any magical powers are abused, the people became hostile immediately towards the death-bearers. Ghosters and Deathwitches, even some Ethermen and others were quick to leave town until the furor died. At a time like this, the Evlans were much discouraged by this reaction, and worse, Dae's story was published in the Treelent Tribune in a rather scorching article complete with a depiction of Eldus Kabe as the villain. His likeness, which was accurate as the handsome rake as he was, was even swooned over by some ladies. As the bored and small-minded society of Treelent fed upon the little dramas that occurred in the lives of the affluent families, the story was sopped up like gravy; sensationalized far beyond its worth and widely talked about. Eldus was made quite infamous for it..

Where Eldus had gone remained a mystery. There was widespread speculation of his whereabouts but nobody knew where he was. The town's commissioner ordered a search, which was fruitless. The Evlans and Figson had nowhere to turn. Figson, who felt utterly responsible for the humiliation and scandal brought upon the Evlans, made himself scarce. He threw himself into his work, and hoped this would pass. In the meantime, he and Arrick conspired at the club, trying to come up with ways to trap and capture the man who had almost won Dae by force.

Dae stepped down from the coach on the corner of the market square and the main street. It was rare she left the family's property these days. But she was out and about with a purpose this fine morning. In her finest woolen redingote of blood red, for the first cooler day of autumn, her mustard gloves and midnight blue bonnet, she looked her part as the daughter of an extremely rich man. She clutched her reticule and looked up at the four-story building's façade. On a marble plate affixed into the mortar of the stone and brick portico, the words "Ghellick and Yaymes" were etched and gilded in a stylish script.

She fortified herself with a great big sigh, and climbed the three steps, pushing open the door into the round lobby of the law firm. To her left and right were towering double doors that were closed at present. Before her on the right was a large stairway leading up to a stack of three broad mezzanines, one atop the other like a beautiful cake. And to her left was a long table with three young assistants at work. They were sorting through stacks of papers, marking them and making lists. Not one of the three young boys could have been more than sixteen. The eldest looked up at her entrance, and elbowed the next, who did the same for the third, and the three of them bowed clumsily. They all three wore black suits of clothes, save for the pop of white at their collars, cuffs and stockings. Two went back to sorting, the first one smiled at her.

"Welcome Miss. May I perhaps be of assistance?" Dae nodded and reached into her reticule, withdrawing a card with her name on it.

"I am here to see if Mr. Figson Howkes is present and available to be seen?" The boy nodded.

"I believe he is in his office. I will see if he will see you. If I may," the boy reached out and took the card. He wended his way around the table, and then stopped before her. "It may take a moment. Please feel free to sit there, if you would Miss." He pointed to a lavish deep wine-colored sofa of tufted leather. There were two, one on each side of the entranceway. She nodded and sat down, clutching her reticule on her lap, looking around with interest.

He bounded up the stairs and disappeared off of the first mezzanine. One of the doors on her right opened, and a young woman emerged carrying a stack of papers. She was dressed in a black jumper-style gown over a long-sleeved white blouse with a stiff ruffed collar. Her hair was pulled tightly and twisted onto the back of her head in a practical do, and she wore no embellishments except a pair of fetching pince-nez spectacles pinched onto the bridge of her long, elegant nose. She plopped a pile of papers on the table where the boys toiled, and picked up a tidier stack from the other side. Before gliding back in a rustle of thick linen into the room where four other clerks bustled, she slowed to assess Dae with a critical sweep of the eye, raising her brow and pursing her lips as if in disapproval of her. She stepped through the open doorway, and as soon as her train was clear, the door was closed behind her. Dae smirked to herself, and sighed.

Just as this occurred, the flash of white stockings and the clatter of youthful feet on the stairs drew her attention, and the boy stopped midway down and gestured for her to come up. "He will see you immediately," he called. Dae rose to her feet and moved lithely across the lobby to the stairs, and she followed the young fellow up to the second floor. He led her to an office just off the main concourse, and showed her in.

Figson was hanging over some papers with two clerks at his side. He was dipping his quill into the inkwell, against which Dae's card was carefully propped. He looked up to smile at her and gestured for her to come in and sit. He scribbled a few more things, rocked the blotter over his writing, and then handed off the papers to each of the clerks. They exited and closed the door. He tossed the quill into the pot and gave Dae a sheepish smile.

"Miss Evlan, I would never have expected to see you here in a million years," he said with a tentative, shy smile. She returned his smile and tilted her head.

"I came with a purpose. Oh, well, two purposes, perhaps," she explained. He leaned back into his tall leather chair and clutched his hands on his chest, looking at her expectantly.

"I shall begin by saying thank you. Thank you for expeditiously securing information to help indict Mr. Kabe. Without that, I may still be engaged to him," she said. "I didn't get a chance to talk to you after all that, so I thought I would begin by saying it. I also," she added, "wish to thank you for helping Renna win that writing slope. She has been jealous of the one Kallenback sent me. As much as I dislike the man, I cannot help but covet the slope. It's the most beautiful thing I own. I know Renna wanted it fiercely, and when she won that new one, well, all I can say is thank you on that end. You are *so* good to us all, Mr. Howkes." Figson shook his head.

"But before you say anything, I would like to broach the true reason for my visit. And it is something that is important, and I must know." She paused, and took a deep breath. "I beg you do not speak until I am done, for I am already having difficulty even bringing myself to ask this," she sighed.

"Of course, Miss Evlan."

"I know that my behavior the evening of the possession was unquestionably awful. My mother's was as well, and she didn't even have my excuse. I am tremendously ashamed of what happened, and the sense of my powerlessness is heavy and humiliating to me.

But I cannot bear to think that somehow, Mr. Howkes, that you might have been... disappointed in me. In my family. My mother's deference to Mr. Kabe still shames me. You have been so distant and absent of late, I can only suspect that your esteem for me... for all of us has diminished because of what took place,"

"Miss Evla..."

"No, let me finish," she said. "I must then own that I would be very sad to learn that this was the case, for you are very much missed at Highrocks. I have come to ascertain as to why you have chosen to abandon us as a family, so that I and the rest of us no longer dwell on it with such regret," she concluded. "You are part of our family, Mr. Howkes," she added swiftly, her cheeks reddening.

Figson gazed at her in incredulity. Her eyes were misting over with the threat of tears, and her chin was trembling. He could scarce believe it. Arrick had not mentioned any distress from his absence. But Arrick was also not always very observant. Figson shook his head and sighed. Her control of her emotions was fraying.

"Oh, Miss Evlan...." he said with a tone of sincere sympathy. The affection in his voice made the tears roll out onto her freckled cheeks. He stood and circled his desk, kneeling before her and putting his hand on hers. "I am so sorry that you would think that my absence would have anything to do with you or your mother. You did nothing wrong. Nothing at all." She hiccupped, and searched her reticule for a kerchief, which she daubed onto her eyes.

"I fear the distance was entirely because of my own sense of responsibility, Miss Evlan," he confessed. "I have blamed myself for Mr. Kabe's trespasses against your family. He would never have known who you were at all, if it weren't for me. And you never would have suffered the embarrassment and the scandal if it weren't for his grudge against me." Dae let a sob of relief escape and she shook her head, trying to speak. "No, allow me to finish," he said with a mocking, stern tone. She half smiled and dabbed her face again. "As long as he remains free, I feel that I must continue to remain remote from you. He saw that I..." he paused, and then mustered up his resolve. "He saw that I *cherish* you, Miss Evlan, and that would be the only way he could truly hurt me would be to hurt you. If I stay away, then maybe he will stay away too." Dae then succumbed to her sobs, her kerchief over her mouth to muffle the sound of it.

Figson patted her hand gently. When her sobs were under control, she put her kerchief down and put her other hand on his, sandwiching his fingers between her own. She looked into his eyes with a lingering, telling gaze. Figson picked up her hand and put it to his lips. He held them there for a moment, his eyes contemplative. When he lowered them, he wrapped her hand in his and spoke.

"I know that this is not the ideal venue for such declarations, Miss Evlan, but I fear if I do not say it now, I may never say it. I have come to love you over these years. In such a way that I have shaped my life to make myself worthy of you," he rambled. She blinked, her eyes widening. "I may not be handsome, or dashing. I am not high-born or titled. But I know that I would do anything to secure your happiness, Miss Evlan. No. Dae. I will call you Dae. Please tell me you would honor me by agreeing to be my wife. I would understand if it is awkward for you, and I would never begrudge you if you could no…"

"Oh, Figson, why did it take so long for you to ask!?" she exclaimed, interrupting him. She took possession of her hands and placed them on each side of his face, gazing with undeniable affection into his eyes. "I love this face. There is nothing that isn't handsome about it. There is nothing that isn't gentlemanly and wonderful about you, Figson," she told him. "I may not have always loved you like I do now. But I realized at the cotillion ball, that I cannot imagine being without you. Of course I would consent to a marriage to you. I could marry nobody else but you. If you never asked me, I would always be alone."

She then leaned forward and gently brushed her lips on his; placing upon him the sweetest kiss he could have ever hoped for. When she withdrew, his eyes too were glossed in tears of joy.

"I haven't formally asked your father permission to marry you," he suddenly said.

"I doubt he will resent you for that," she replied. "He likes you very much."

"I like him too." She smiled.

"Now, you must come to dinner tonight. I was commanded by mother that if I did find you, that I should invite you, for Renna and mother and father all have missed you. But you are welcome to simply enjoy the day with us in its entirety. You should leave with me now, unless you have work to do." Figson smiled and stood, holding her hands.

"I have a few more papers to sign, and we can go together. I will ride up behind the coach; if you would wait but a moment or two." She nodded.

Basking in the light of her affection, he sat at his desk and scratched out some more work with his quill, glancing up now and again to ascertain that she was indeed truly there, and truly smiling lovingly upon him as promised one.

A few days after the newly engaged couple made the announcement to the family, and they were toasted and celebrated by them in turn, the Treelent Tribune published a small missive about the engagement in the paper. It read:

Lately, the young woman recently reported to have been wickedly wiled and worked by spectral means into an engagement to an iniquitous deathwitch; has entered into a consenting engagement with an esteemed young lawyer of this city's most prestigious firm. Sources say that the engagement took place near Highrocks, and that the family, after the tragic possession that nearly cost a fortune, celebrated the event with iced pear wine and blue pumpkin cakes. The TT extends its deepest well-wishes on the newly engaged couple. They will make a stylish and welcome addition to the townhouse neighborhood of Nettle Street.

These words were absorbed over a hearty breakfast served to a Mr. Havel Mood at the Seaspring Inn in Kaberly, about thirty miles up the coast from Treelent. Mr. Mood, a man who looked remarkably and suspiciously like the block prints of the infamous wicked deathwitch, Eldus Kabe, stared at the article with narrowed eyes, and red ears. The paper crumpled in a gripped fist and then was hurled violently into the nearby fireplace. The act startled several other diners sharing the common dining room with this gentleman. Sumptuous breakfast left untouched, the Seaspring Inn was soon left in the wake of a horse and curricle, which was headed towards Treelent at top speed.

"Lately, the young woman recently reported to have been *wickedly wiled,*" Dae read out in a singsong voice, holding the paper aloft. She giggled and read on, her audience of her father, mother, sister and affianced was all humor as she mockingly read the article for them all to hear. As she did, she experienced a surge of dizziness she had never felt before. It started in her head, and then washed over her body until her knees buckled. She collapsed into a heap, her gown ballooning and then settling onto her, the paper fluttering to the ground by her extended arm. The family rose in alarm and fell to her side, hands gripping her as she breathed shallowly, tried to speak, and then spit up some wine onto the rug. Her body went into a violent seizure and she shuddered, her muscles constricting violently and then relaxing. She fell deathly still.

"SALTS!" Figson shouted, gathering her upper body up onto his knees. He touched her throat and then gripped her wrist. His face was filled with terror. Naya fumbled to find her bottle of smelling salts, and succeeded, pulling them from her deep petticoat pocket.

Figson applied them under Dae's nose to no avail. She was unconscious. "Call the damned physician, please!" he barked. Arrick was already getting to his feet when there was the sound of another thump. They turned to see Renna on the ground as well, seizing.

Figson's devastation was complete. He threw himself onto the slight form on the bed, weeping into the cool, pale nape of her neck. He and Arrick both knew this was not what the physician claimed it was.

"Avasanne is such a scourge for the medical community. We are so powerless against it. There are no grey areas, there is only one way or the other. You die within hours of exposure, or you languish in a catatonic state for weeks. There are no cures, no remedies. It is a gamble," the doctor spoke to Arrick and Figson, his arms crossed before him; his shoulders defeated. Naya wept and wept.

"Have they been out walking?"

"Always. Up at the falls just this morning," Naya replied woefully.

"There must have been a growth of the Avasanne. Perhaps if they strayed off the pathways," he said. Naya nodded. "They always forged their own paths. They could have been touched by the plant and never even known it," she blubbered. The doctor nodded regretfully.

"I will speak to the commissioner to have some men set a burn up there, just in case. We cannot have more of those plants popping up like weeds and harming more innocent children," he sighed. "I am very sorry Mr. Evlan, Mr. Figson, Mrs. Evlan, for your loss. Tragic loss indeed. The physician bade his farewells and left the house to notify the death-guide of their passing.

Naya collapsed into a chair, and Figson, bloodshot eyes and wan complexion, looked at Arrick. "I must find a ghoster," he said grimly.

"Why?" Naya exclaimed.

"Because if they were killed by spectral means, the ghoster will tell us."

"They're all gone," Arrick muttered. "The masters of death-arts are all gone."

"I'll find one. He will be able to tell by the spectral wakes in this house if anything untoward occurred."

"I'm glad I'm not the only one suspecting that this wasn't Avasanne."

"It wasn't Avasanne. It was revenge," Figson spat. Arrick bent forward onto his knees and his shoulders began to shake in misery.

"They were my baby girls…" he sobbed.

Figson secured the name of a ghoster from a town about eight miles from Treelent. He sent a message to him using the hawks, and returned the next day to the house, his heart heavy with the knowledge that it contained so little to tempt him to return now. Without Dae, his world was empty. He arrived as the family was making preparations for the interment of Dae and Renna. Arrick, oddly controlled and taciturn, stood by. Figson, filled with only misery, looked on.

Dae and Renna's bodies were swathed in silk by four white-clad aestrals; employed by the death-guide, they were purposed to prepare the bodies for the ceremony of burial and transition. The girls were bent into fetal positions, and placed in their smooth, egg-shaped vessels. The family stood present for the sealing. Figson wept again as the lid closed over Dae's body.

The vessels were lifted by the pall bearers onto the hearse. Naya placed garlands of flowers around the ovoid vessels, and the family followed the slow-moving equipage on foot as the horses drew them towards the family plot to be buried with their ancestors.

The spirit guide was waiting with his two channels by the gaping hole in the earth. The three were clad in blue-black robes. The channels had small round hats on their heads, the guide, a half-circle radiated from his. They had already been at work before the coffins arrived. Around the large earthen hole, a tangle of woven patterns created in colored sands, powders and seeds surrounded the burial site, carefully rendered by the guide and the channels. There was an unfinished portion where the bearers would walk to deliver the vessels to the grave.

The process was long and painful. As the caskets were lowered, all Figson could do was wonder at how small the vessels seemed. Once the two eggs were settled into the earth, the pall bearers drew away, and the guide and channels completed the woven pattern, carefully pouring the media from sacred jars. During the whole process, nobody had spoken a word. Not even the family or Figson.

He stood impassive, watching the three ceremonial guides apply their work. He felt something brush his hand. He glanced down to see Arrick's hand nudging his. He had something in his fingers. Figson took whatever it was, feeling the tickle of fine hair as he slid it into the pocket on the side of his frock coat. He knew immediately what Arrick had given him. He had given him the hair of his daughters. Locks, trimmed from their lifeless bodies.

The gesture of receiving a token taken from the body of a dead person meant only one thing to a deathwitch. Arrick wanted Figson to resurrect his daughters.

The locks of hair contained all the information that was required for the rebuilding of the girls' physical bodies. Their appearance, their age---all that was missing was the spirit that resided within them. Figson wondered if he had it in him to do it. He could not believe that Arrick was sanctioning this idea. It was highly illegal to resurrect the dead. It could be punishable by death. And there was the matter of the family; how it would affect them and their daily lives. The death of the girls was common knowledge. It would certainly make ripples if they were to suddenly reappear.

Both Arrick and Naya were staring at Figson. He sat across from them, clutching each little plait of hair in his hand, each end tied with a small scrap of ribbon. Dae's lighter shade so distinct and recognizable, Renna's darker shiny hair smooth against his thumb.

"I could be sentenced to death for it," he told them. He wasn't objecting, he was only stating a fact. "You too, for initiating the act. You would both be subject to aiding and abetting the crime. They nodded. Arrick frowned.

"It's a risk we are willing to take. It rests entirely on you. We understand if you do not wish to take that risk too. Their lives are more important than ours."

"There is no question for me, Arrick. I will do it regardless. If I am caught, I am caught."

"Eldus is a deathwitch too. One far more practiced than you. He used his powers to possess her, which already has been proven. We need only implicate him once the ghoster arrives. There's a chance that we could be believed," Arrick offered. Figson snorted and sighed heavily. Figson sensed how wrong it was to think this way, but he was beyond grief and pain, and all he could do was nod. He didn't think it was possible. But it was worth a try. He gazed down at the braids in his hand.

"I've never built anything bigger than a cat," he said.

"You will prevail and you will return our girls to us. They were wrongfully taken. Murdered. Please, Figson, I beg you, please;"

Naya began to weep as she supplicated him. "Bring me my babies back."

"They will have no memory of their death," Figson added. "The longer they are dead, the longer the period before their death they will forget. A day of memories will be lost for each day that passes."

"They will remember *nothing*?" Naya exclaimed.

"The memories can be recalled with help from a certain sort of bearer. But the revenant or a guardian must know they have been resurrected and seek out the bearer themselves. We can simply help the girls believe that they never perished. That the Avasanne took the form of the sleeping sickness. It will hopefully prevent them from seeking out the truth," he mumbled. He rubbed his temples and groaned. "We can only pray they never discover the deathmark on their wrists."

Naya sniffed, and drew the back of her hand over her eyes. There was a pall as they sat there in the deathly quiet parlor which had once been such a warm and welcoming space. Even the quality of light had the air of gloom and a bluish hue. For a long spell, nobody said a word. They were each lost in their grief and desperation. The quiet was obliterated by Figson, who dropped his hands and peered at the girls' father. His expression was one of resolve.

"Getting what I need will take time. I'll be surprised if I can have all the preparations I need to do this within six months. Some things are hard to come by." He looked gravely upon Arrick. "If it takes six months, that means they will forget the six months prior to their death; time they spent with you, and…" he suspired sorrowfully; "with me." Arrick leapt upon his words, the optimism rising within him. His face was awash with desperate hope.

"That can be rebuilt if the foundations of that affection is there already, Figson," Arrick pleaded breathlessly. "You can make it like it was. You can marry her as you wished. It may take some doing, some effort to restore the deeper feelings she developed for you these past months. But she already loves you. She always has."

"Sir, there is no need to convince me, I've already decided I am going to do what I can to bring them both back. Whether her feelings for me are reborn or not, her life must be restored. As well as Renna's. But I will do this only on one condition; and that is you do what you must to track down that blaggard, so that he can have his due," Figson's glare became black and baleful, and his fists tightened around the locks of hair. Arrick nodded grimly. The decision had been made. Renna and Dae would be resurrected from the dead, and Figson would be the one to do it.

****

Figson brushed some of the powder from his knee, and straightened himself. He was crouched over the piles of elements he had poured with great care and precision, much like the colored sands and seeds that had decorated the earthen grave the girls' bodies rested in. This was a different application.

Two long, oval wooden basins rested on the brick floor. The wood was smoothened and each had a ring of figures carved along the top inner edge. The basins were filled to the edges with clear, fresh water, the carved figures submerged. The surface still rippled from when Figson poured in a blend of elements from ceremonial jars. Some materials still swirled slowly on the surface, making whorls of powdery shapes on the water.

He poured an interweaving design around the basins in various elemental powders. He eyed the composition; each powder had its own unique colour and texture; its own lightness or heaviness, its own volatility and state. With his finger, he drew some figures into the final shapes, blending one type of material into the next.

The weave of materials and the mounds under the water in the basins included plain carbon, phosphorous, sulfur and calcium, various metals finely ground. These were the essential elements of a living being—touching the air from which it would draw life, and submerged in water which would give the elements form.

Acquiring many of these materials posed a challenge. Several were illegal to possess unless under permit by the ministry of the Spectral Arts, because they were used mostly for this unlawful act. The ceremonial jars were obtained through illicit sources. With Arrick's money, it was a challenge overcome, and Figson's extensive list of needs was fulfilled. The materials arrived on ships from myriad locations, hidden in larger shipments, difficult if not impossible to track. Just under twelve weeks of waiting, and he had what he needed. In the cellars of Highrocks, he gathered the provisions he needed. When he had everything, including the tubs that were custom-made by an aged ghoster and carpenter; and transported to the house in the dark of night; he painstakingly arranged the items and ingredients according to the traditions of the early resurrection rites; reading them from a book that was over three hundred years old. He consulted the texts repeatedly to ensure he had done it just as directed.

Figson had vigilantly measured each ingredient ~~out~~ according to the strict diagrams. He wrote in the figures into the dusts that would summon the magic he needed. And when he was done with that, he straightened himself and extracted from his pockets the locks of hair. He gently placed one on the surface water of each basin, watching them darken with water and then sink down to rest on top of the submerged powders. He stepped back. With a trembling breath, he whispered:

"Well, girls. Let's bring you home."

It had been years since Figson had dabbled with his abilities. It wasn't something one could forget, but performing the magic of a deathwitch took a powerful physical toll, no matter how small the task. But Figson's state of mind was not even remotely close to considering what this could cost him. All he wanted was to see Dae's freckled face again, even if he would never see the look of love in her eyes again as she gazed upon him. All that mattered was that she would be alive again. And Renna too. All he wanted to spite Eldus and undo what he had done. He wanted to take away the hurt his old friend had inflicted upon him and the family. It was all the passion he needed to fuel not one, but two resurrections.

****

The ghoster had an interesting tale to tell Arrick and Figson; after he stood over the girls' graves, and ventured around the property. They waited for him at a public house, while he performed his assessment; not conversing, but instead sitting quietly, clutching their goblets of ale; lost in thought. The ghoster joined them after his lengthy survey, and ordered an ale as the two gentleman had. In the darkened, low-ceilinged public house, there were only a few souls present besides the three. An old man hunched over his ale, murmuring to himself, and two younger fellows talking quietly by the fire. There was nobody nearby to hear their conversation. The ghoster was a wiry fellow, with a pate of thinning hair and wild muttonchops. He had watery, pinkened eyes and a large red nose. He wrapped his bony fingers around the clumsy pewter goblet and acknowledged each man with a glance.

His findings were described for the two men. Figson looked on bitterly, Arrick gravely. The girls had been forcefully possessed by a type of apparition called a life-thief. These were malevolent and difficult to control. They were known to settle into living victims and to drain them of their life force. Like wraiths, these were never spirits that occupied the living world. They were native to the shadethers, and were eager to supply their world with broken souls to feed on.

They were so rare that they were thought to be legend in many places. The symptoms of the possession looked exactly like death by Avasanne. The ghoster snorted through his nose and said: "I suspect that most Avasanne deaths are cases of life-thievery, but nobody really knows the difference anymore. I suppose you could tell by the type of person it was that died," he conceded. Life-thieves sought particular types of victims. Namely they hunted for people who were morally corrupt. The common threat to a naughty child was to threaten them with life thieves if they did bad things. These nasty ghosts were attracted to despicable souls. They fed upon them. "Nobody would suspect that these girls were killed in such a manner; as they were both fair and innocent creatures, so there was no other reason to think it was anything other than Avasanne," he added. "Your suspicious nature proved correct," he told Arrick. "I never would have guessed myself, to be honest." He paused and drank from his mug.

He then shook his head. "I was dubious initially, that the deaths were anything but illness. But now it makes sense, now that I've felt the traces of life-thieves. It's an uncommon scenario, but it is one that is logical given the evidence I sensed. The second girl died because of an oversight. The deathwitch summoned one life thief, and ended up with two," he exclaimed. He held up two of his gnarled digits; his black eyes shining, his voice gravelly. "And that is not an uncommon occurrence when the life thief is misused. I must reiterate; it's rare. In all my days I've never seen it like this first-hand. I've only heard it during my apprenticeship days."

Arrick and Figson did not respond. They merely looked upon him with expectation. Arrick sipped from his drink loudly, his eyes locked on the man's drawn face. He continued.

"It's hard enough to summon one of those things, and to struggle it into your victim. A life thief is like a wild beast. You have to secure a firm hold on it and force it into a body. They normally choose their *own* victims. It is against the natural order of things to force one into a body it has not chosen. It takes a great deal of strength to do it, so your deathwitch is one of significant strength. But he wasn't one who was sufficiently prepared.

"You see, once it's in there, it's there for the duration. But to use it to inflict harm on an innocent person, well that's just plain mad," he hissed, squeezing the back of his neck with his hand. "I've come to the conclusion, based on these fading residues I have assessed, that a second life-thief came for your murderer."

Arrick's thick brows shot up in astonishment, and Figson straightened up in his seat. They waited for the proprietor of the public house to replace their goblets, looking at one another in silence until the man drew away. Then the ghoster continued, sipping first from his fresh goblet of ale, and wiping the foam from his lips with his sleeve.

"This kind of murder is a trespass that could *only* result in that," he whispered, his hands rising to pantomime his next missive. "He has one spirit set inside of his victim, he has accomplished this, and then suddenly he is confronted by the presence of another. Well, what do you do? If you have the power to draw and restrain spirits, you wrestle it into someone else before it gets you. I'm confident that this is what happened."

"Renna…" Arrick muttered bitterly. "He killed Renna to save himself."

"The shadether has marked him. It's only a matter of time before one of those things gets him. Your deathwitch is on the run. He may be for some time. The spirit world does not much tolerate abuse like that." He dropped his hands and drank from his ale, looking at it as if it too boggled his mind.

"Can you find any traces where he might have gone?" Arrick asked.

"I am a ghoster, sir, with all due respect. My specialty is with the dead. You best find a good scent hound for this living man. However, I suspect if he isn't careful, he will end up under my realm of expertise sooner or later. You don't do what he did with native shadether spirits and get away with it," he replied decisively.

"I'd rather be sure," Arrick growled. Figson nodded, his hands gripping his goblet tighter. The ghoster's eyes fell to the table searchingly and there was an awkward silence. He then studied each face across from him, and at length, he spoke.

"He knows that the life-thieves are after him now. So he can take measures to avoid them or derail them," Figson added.

"Well, there is one thing you can do, but I won't do it for you, and if asked, I never told you this," the ghoster leaned over the table and whispered these words. "When the dead are resurrected, the wraiths that hunt the revenants to bring them back to the shadethers; they can be useful. Ghosters don't have to destroy them right away, if they know what they are doing." He stopped, as if questioning himself on this matter, but continued, with an air of hesitation.

"A wraith is created when the spirit's connection to the shadether is severed. A wraith is a remnant of the spirit you have taken away into the living world, and it is the spirit's counterpart in the shadether. If the wraith succeeds in returning the spirit to the death realm, it merges with it again to make it whole," he explained. He leaned back on his side of the tall bench, and sighed.

"The wraith is an anchor in many ways. But the wraith is still part of the spirit of the person and they possess all the memories lost when the spirit crosses. And along with those memories, there are the connections to the living people close to them or those who had an influence in their life; that include a connection to their murderers if they exist. This was commonly done in the times of the Druids. To answer the unanswerable. Now, naturally it is unlawful," he said with care.

"*If* a resurrection happened, and I am only speaking theoretically, you could snare the wraith as soon as it first materializes . Trap it, and use ghosting skills to find the spiritual connection you seek, and make it lead you to your killer. But that is only if there is resurrection," he added quickly. "And that is unlawful, as I said," he blurted, laughing uncomfortably. Figson's eyes narrowed and his lips formed a hard thin line.

"Your best bet is to count on your life-thieves to do what they do best. It's possible they already have. He is powerful, if he did what he did, which means he could be fending them off. If you're looking, you might even find a trail of supposed Avasanne deaths that will lead you to him—as he sheds his pursuers into the bodies of strangers to divert them." The two men were stone still, both clutching their ales.

"Thank you, sir for your diligent services," Arrick suddenly blurted. He fished about in his pocket, and reached across the table. The ghoster accepted the thick silver coins for his services, watching them click into his hand with overt satisfaction. Content with the generous payment, he stood, bowed deeply and put on his hat. He left the men alone at the table in the public house. They gazed at one another in incredulity.

"I must find a ghoster willing to trap those wraiths. A man willing to be complicit in a crime," Arrick muttered. He pinched his chin, and his eyes wandered. Then Figson spoke.

"There is a person I know. But it is not a man. But for me, she would do this."

"Who would that be?" Arrick replied.

"She isn't a practicing ghoster, she is a ship's captain."

"Your mother?"

"Indeed sir," Figson retorted. He picked up his ale and drained it.

"No. I will involve nobody else from our families," he declared. Figson shook his head.

"Every day that passes, the more we lose of their recent memories, Arrick. We must get them back soon, and my mother will help. She is a trustworthy, honorable soul who would volunteer herself if she were sitting here. I am going to ask for her help. That… That soulless scum must be punished." Arrick pondered on this for a good spell, and then with a nod he conceded, lifting up his goblet to Figson.

"To justice, then."

"To justice," Figson replied. They toasted and drained their cups. Figson rose to his feet, and put on his hat too.

"I'll go home now. I'm hoping the final shipment of metal powders will have arrived, and we can get this bit over with."

Arrick had always been fascinated by Figson's mother. He had met her once when he was at the shipyards with Figson and the Jezebel was at port. Zillig women were still somewhat atypical on Garvash. Although the western ways had long been melding with the central isle culture, this one aspect was slower to grow than others. But women were beginning to embrace this new gender role, and testing the waters of pursuing lives as businesswomen and professionals. The men were even more reluctant to accept that other men might choose simpler lives and become Emzilla, men walking as women.

Mrs. Howkes was a beautiful woman to begin with, statuesque and elegant, with strong, determined features and a powerful confidence in her carriage. She interacted with her peers with the expected decisiveness and certainty of a ship's captain. Arrick was not often confronted by women who were the opposite of soft spoken, who did not apologize constantly for taking up space, or shrink into the background in the presence of men. She took charge of the dialogue from their first moment of meeting; she dug right into the conversation with Arrick, and gazed at him directly. He seemed derailed by the dark lashed, expectant eyes and her tall bicorne dancing with snowy feathers. She shook his hand with a confident grip, and listened intently to his praise of her son.

"He is a fine young man," she agreed. "I hope you treat him with the esteem that you would offer your own child, Mr. Evlan," she warned him with a jesting smile. "The Jezebel is a fine merchant ship, but she is amply supplied with weapons. They're mostly for pirates; but also for use on people who abuse my son." He laughed in surprise, and shook his head.

"No violence is necessary. I esteem this boy very much."

He had been much taken by her manner and openness. It was extremely refreshing. However his second meeting with her lacked the joviality, and instead was weighed down by the very gravity of what they were doing. As Figson had told him, she was more than willing to be part of this. She arrived at the house in her lay clothes. It was hardly any different to what Arrick wore. He was briefly distracted by that, but then the knowledge of what they were doing returned and he focused instead on the strange scene Figson had assembled in the cellar of his home.

"There will always be a tear in the shades here, Arrick," Mrs. Howkes said informally. "So you might have some spectral activity here now."

"I am neither concerned about ghosts or their effect on my home's value, please do not worry yourself on the matter," he grunted brusquely. Both mother and son acknowledged him with a nod. Mrs. Evlan reached out and took her husband's arm. He patted her hand and sighed.

"We are obligated to disclose the consequences of a resurrection," Mrs. Howkes replied. "That is all." Arrick bowed shallowly and looked away, examining the space the young fellow had prepared. A bristle of standing candelabras encircled the darkened portion of the cavernous cellars. This was only one of the many alcoves made for cask storage. In the center of the floor, two long basins he had to have made per Figson's specifications; long, narrow canoe-like vessels both filled to the brim with clean water. The bottom of each basin was covered in a layer of white and grey mottled sand of some sort, with blots of darker material poured atop. He spied a flicker of color from the ribbons that bound the locks of hair together. They rested under the water as well. The water was not still. It moved subtly in the darkness, catching the reflection of the myriad candles.

Around these basins were other powders and grains, intermingled in a knotted design that was beautiful in its own right, moving in a figure eight around each basin; connecting the two. Figson removed his frock and his mother took it, laying it over a barrel of spirits they were using as a table. She brought him a black robe which she lifted onto his shoulders, and then he did the same for her once she removed her frock coat. It was a silent process, the gravity of the moment hung heavily around them, and their small movements seemed loud. Even their breathing could be heard. The water still rippled without cause. Figson understood this was a sign of the figures and markings drawing in the death powers. It was a signal that he had done his job efficiently and prepared the ceremony properly.

Figson moved to the far end of the alcove, at the foot of these basins. There was a circle in the design of the knot just to accommodate him. He stepped into it, and sank down onto a cross legged position and arranged his robes as to not disturb the powdered lines encircling him.

"Mr. and Mrs. Evlan, I recommend you sit over there, and please remain silent," he whispered. Arrick nodded, and guided Naya to the alcove across from the one glowing with candle light, and they rested in wine crates.

"I am beginning, mother," he declared. The dark haired lady nodded gravely and settled in just at the edge of the alcove, eyes trained on the shimmering water. Figson closed his eyes and searched for the sensations he once knew well. He found them where they had always been, furled in the front of his skull, prickly and anxious, as if the powers had been waiting all these years for this one moment.

It felt like that moment when one is transitioning into sleep, when there is a vague awareness of the waves of slumber lapping into the waking mind. The deathwitch inside him, woken and aware, blossomed out across his consciousness and washed his senses with its buzzing presence. When his eyes opened again, his vision was painted with the shadether.

The ordinary world rested behind a scrim of deep water colors, the air was heavy and languid, the very movement of the world seemingly slowed. Within the undulating currents of the shadether, he witnessed slips of grey and black, slipping through the denseness like porpoises; gathering around the resonance made by the presence of the deathwitch.

The thick ether trembled as Mrs. Howkes' vision also disturbed the veil. Both mother and son looked like ghosts in the light of shadethers. The only clear objects to be seen were the two small plaited strands of hair, which looked as if they glowed against the murky backdrop. Pure connections to death, they acted like beacons. As the deathwitch watched, the spirits gathered and schooled, circling these beacons as soon as he opened the way for them to shine inside the shadethers.

The circle of curious spirits began to gather and concentrate around each relic, each one seeking the familiarity of the manifestation. As the spirits gathered, and grew closer, he began to see glimpses of a faint glow. The light shimmered stronger, the closer the apparitions swam around the beacons. The relics were bathing the spirits that had once owned them in their light. The harder Figson concentrated, the brighter the two little slips of sinuous matter became. The other gathering spirits, sensing no familiarity to these objects began to fall away.

Figson remained fast, forcing his entire consciousness in maintaining a clear path between the locks of hair and the shadethers. When the individual gleaming spirits were within an acceptable distance, Figson lifted his hands and drew pockets of the waking world into the ethers, fully exposing the relics to the spirits. He waiting until the spirits slipped through them, to immerse themselves into the objects to which they belonged. The moment they did, he snapped the pockets closed, and trapped them in the living world.

The shadethers withdrew like theatrical curtains as Figson, still keeping the spirits contained, returned his mind to the living world. There, his mother waited. Here, she could relieve him of the job of containing the spirits, until he could encapsulate them into their new bodies. The relics of hair, soaked in the basins, were now more than just parts of the dead. They were now vessels for the spirits of their owners.

He felt as if someone was lifting a heavy weight from his body, and saw his mother assume the task of restraining Dae and Renna, and keeping their spirits bound to their relics. It would allow him to now do the hard part. He stretched his neck by rolling his head, and then with care, he extended his arms and flattened his hands, lowering his open palms to the edge of the design that surrounded him and the basins. With a two heavy gulps of air, he dug his hands into the powders, and his body stiffened as the power within him immediately flowed through the powders; which acted as a conductor, and follow the intricate pathways poured on the ground.

The powders immediately began to react to the stream of magic flowing through them. Some lines smoked, others made of sands and metals melted and pooled. The alcove filled with acrid smoke that floated over the water. Dusts and particles, ash and embers hissed on the water surface. Inside the basins, the water heated as pulses of magic radiated in towards the basins; directed by the designs that enclosed them. The piles of material under the surface began to seethe. The braids were swallowed up by the moving sands.

Inside of Figson's head, the process was neat and tidy; unlike the reek and chaos that encircled his physical body. The elements resonated, they moved, they were shaped by the intricate dance of power that bound them. The braids were being disintegrated, particle by particle, turned into spirit-imbued matter that was roiled into the morass of creation, washed into the blend of the physical and the magical until they were nothing more than part of the growing whole.

They provided the template; the information that the magic needed to assemble the puzzle. To draw the elements together to resemble what the relics had once been part of. Figson's hands burned against the elements, the stone flags blackened beneath pools of glass and metal and fire, intermingling. The basins swallowed the emissions from this fiery blend, the smoke moving as if sucked into the water. The water boiled turbid. But, as each moment passed the particles that clouded it were being amassed, gathered and ordered beneath the roiling surface. The layers were wrapped one atop the other, bones, muscle, sinew and organs; assembled from the raw materials Figson had poured from urns into the water and onto the stone. Figson could see in his mind's eye, the transformation of these gruesome figures as they grew more and more like the girls they had lost.

When their pale, delicate skin had invested itself onto the slim, waify forms, and their hair and fingernails had finally been knit to their bodies; there again were the girls they knew, resting like the dead in the basins. The majority of the water was now part of them, the nude figures rested in puddles of sooty, oily water. Figson lifted his reddened hands, the skin in some places already rising up into great blisters. The heat dissipated, and the glowing hot materials began to cool.

Careful not to step on the molten materials, Figson's mother gingerly stepped between the basins, and bent down. She touched each body in turn and nodded to her son with a sweet, subtle, victorious smile. She then took two large towels from under her arm and covered each one.

"The shovel please," she gestured to Arrick, who straightened himself, and scurried to fetch what she asked for, approaching with trepidation. "Scrape away that stuff. Put it over there. Make a path so you and your wife can get them out of here. They won't wake for several days.". He nodded and did as she bade, throwing the partially molten materials into a corner and away from the basins.

Figson struggled to his feet. Weakened by the process, he stumbled from the circle that had bound him, and staggered out of the alcove. He leaned heavily against the wall and looked at the face in each basin. With an elated laugh he collapsed onto his knees, his burnt hands clawed before him; and then hunched over in wracking sobs of relief and joy.

It took only a day for the wraiths to arrive. Mrs. Howkes waited with calculated patience, sitting in a wingback between the girls' beds, watching with her ghoster sight. She held her vessels close. Naya doted and fussed over her daughters, weeping almost every time she saw one of their fingers twitch, or she heard one of them sigh. They slept deeply.

Wraith hauntings were often violent ones. These came early and that was a blessing. They arrived in a blast of shadether winds and with shrieks that would have terrified Imelda. They flung objects and roared about in inky slips of apparitions. Mrs. Howkes stood her ground and did her work. Arm out, vessels clutched with their charmed stoppers dangling from the bottlenecks in silver chains, she was ready for them. First one, then the other, she wrestled into the vials, her teeth clenched and her brow set in a furious slant. Ghosters hated wraiths, and her desire to disperse them into nothing but smoke was strong. But they had a job to do first. She trapped them in the little silver amphorae, ran from the room, and burst into the office where Arrick and Figson bided their time.

"Got the bloody bastards," she declared with a feral, victorious grin.

Mrs. Howkes was no gentle creature, that Mr. Evlan learned the moment she extricated one of the wraiths from the vessel and suspended it in a binding spell. The slick, viscous thing twisted and writhed against its bonds to no avail. Mrs. Howkes stood before it, her hands on her hips, in her shirtsleeves, her eyes focused on the struggling entity. Her conversation with it was silent. But the others looked on regardless, curious in the case of the Evlans; for Figson, it was merely a desire to be present. He was weakened and frail. He'd spent the past several hours vomiting and retching. His hands, bound in bandages, trembled and he could barely stand. He sat in a tall chair made of willow withes, which had two wooden wheels and a bar on it so that he could be pushed wherever he needed.

Mrs. Evlan had swathed him in blankets and ordered that he remain at the family residence, and be cared for under her supervision. His assigned caretaker, Mr. Evlan's senior valet, was at present fetching another batch of rich broth, which was the only thing he could keep down for now. He refused the care of a physician, fearing that their actions would be discovered too soon. There was a silent understanding that their time was limited. As long as Dae and Renna were returned to the world, it was all that mattered.

Their story had been formulated should their crime be discovered. Mrs. Evlan was to have been absent, visiting a relative in Rellemstad while the girls were ill. She hurried to return for their burial, only to discover them resurrected. Mr. Evlan insisted she have no part in the story, and no responsibility for the decision or the actions that brought the girls back. Arrick and Figson would take their chances.

Dae and Renna were still cataleptic, resting comfortably in their beds, garbed in fresh night gowns. They were attended to by their new nurse. Like Figson, they too required time to mend and recover from the trauma of a resurrection.

Figson watched his mother from the depth of his darkened sockets, his sallow skin looking almost grey in the dimness of the office. There, they were guaranteed the privacy they needed. Figson's mother was the way he remembered her before her captaining days, when she worked as a Ghoster. This was when he was very young. Before he was sent to school.

She always had a girlish glow whenever she used her powers. The air of confidence and contentment she emanated while practicing was the reason why he wanted to work as a deathwitch when he realized he had those abilities. But his mother never made much money working as a ghoster. As a woman, and a Zillig, she only faced more difficulty in a part of the island nations that was relatively quiet when it came to spectral activity. His father and mother both agreed that his abilities, although a gift, would not serve him well in providing him a fruitful living, in spite of his being a man. She gave them up so they could send Figson to a good school, as Ryus had most wanted.

Figson could not help but notice how much happier his mother seemed doing what was natural to her. Even now, while she tightened the bonds harshly around the wraith, and her brow slanted down as she silently bombarded it with her will; she looked comfortable in her element.

The wraith was a fighter. Figson imagined it was Dae's . He smiled wanly, saddened that she would not remember the moments when they finally found the place in their relationship where they both understood the feelings shared by the other. He hoped they would be able to reach that place again. He didn't hold much hope, as the realization came upon him that he had indeed committed a crime punishable by death. He hoped the plan Mr. Evlan had of indicting the man who had murdered them would work. He couldn't imagine why anyone would murder and then resurrect someone. He held onto the expectation that nobody would ask that question and concentrate only on the madness of any person who would summon life-thieves.

Mrs. Howkes reached out her hand, holding in it the silver vessel that had imprisoned the wraith. It had calmed, and now slipped into the bottle without being coerced. She stopped it and handed it to Mr. Evlan. "This one will tell you where to find the deathwitch.

He is in the city. This wraith will take you to him for the price of his life. He will take him back to the shadether in place of your daughter. That is what it bargained in order to continue to exist. The other one, I will destroy. But only after you've found your quarry." Mr. Evlan took the vial and gazed at it for a moment. It represented another crime that would happen by his hands. He did not look pleased, but he looked resolved.

"So be it," he said. "How will it guide me."

"Keep it in your hand. The wraith will pull you towards the murderer." Mrs. Evlan began to weep, and her husband rubbed her arm, and comforted her in quiet. Mrs. Howkes put on her frock coat and adjusted her collars and cravat in the small mirror before turning to her son, delicately touching his cheek.

"I'll be by tomorrow," she said softly, her warm eyes on him. He nodded once, and she bowed curtly to the Evlans before exiting.

"I'm off then, Mr. Evlan declared. "Sooner better than later." There was a curt finality to his words. He kissed his wife, and held her face, giving her a meaningful look. She wiped her tears and he dropped his hands. "Take care of Figs." He looked to Figson once, with a grateful smile, and followed Mrs. Howkes out the door. Mrs. Evlan circled behind Figson and sighed, gripping the bar of the wheeled chair.

"Well, it's just you and me, Figson," she exhaled. "Let's see where Fenrid has gone with that broth of yours," she sighed. Figson shrank into his swaddling and emitted a sigh of his own. Deep down, in spite of the joy of having the girls back in the arms of the living world, he could not help but mourn how large a price they would pay for it all. He wished he had the strength to be there when Arrick met with Eldus, for he wished he could make him pay even more for the mess he made of so many lives.

****

Arrick sat down in the chair by the fire, and crossed his legs, reaching for his pipe. He filled the bowl with the fragrant herbs, and used a long stick to light it from the hearth. The silence was heavy. The sound of the clock ticking was almost unnaturally loud and irritating to the two occupants of the room.

Figson didn't have the strength to ask anything. But he was filled with questions. Arrick had been gone for almost two days. He returned shortly after Figson and Naya had breakfasted. The girls had yet to wake. The house was a somber place after Arrick left. There was a sense of the inevitable, and the girls not waking was worrying Naya. Figson trusted that they would wake. Having performed a dual resurrection might have stretched his abilities, and likely increased the work that needed to be completed by the lingering magic in their bodies. He would not be able to heal fully until their bodies were ready to awaken to their new life. It was his magic; his very essence that continued to sustain and repair them. Until they were finished healing, he was consigned to his weakness.

He languished in his rolling chair, unable to absorb much food. He hunched like an old man in a wrapping of blankets. Naya saw to his care, and in spite of every comfort being met, he was still in tremendous pain and quite weak. His hands, the blisters drained and the dead skin shed, looked awful; raw open sores, inflamed and tender. He kept them covered, and held them to his chest gingerly; for everything he did hurt.

He spent the time when Arrick was away by Dae's side, staring at the flawless skin on her familiar face, with its precious spray of freckles he so adored. For the moment, both of the girls looked still and waxen, like facsimiles of the originals. But once their spirits woke inside them, they would look alive. He was certain of this. With each passing day, their looks improved. Colour to their cheeks, more depth to their breath, more serenity in their rest.

This morning he took breakfast in the drawing room with Naya. He weakly sipped from his spoonful of milky oats. The honey and cream tasted lovely, but he could already feel his stomach rejecting the warm sustenance. He fought to keep it down, his wobbly, bandaged hand pausing just over the bowl, just close enough for the spoon to rattle quietly on it as his hand trembled.

Naya had eaten a little, but mostly stared at her food. She was still in her dressing gown, a large frilly cap covering her hair. She looked over at him and then jumped a little when Arrick burst into the room. He poured himself some tea and sat down next to his wife at the table, and slid his hand over to squeeze hers. The look they exchanged was all the confirmation Figson needed that Eldus now belonged to the shadethers.

Arrick revealed a deep gash on his lower arm when he and Figson were alone in the smoking room. He had changed into a banyan and put on some slippers, and was chillingly silent for at least an hour. The clock ticked, the room seemed to turn a grey blue from the clouds of smoke, and still he did not speak. Figson lifted his quivering hand to his mouth. He was grateful for the sipper, for it prevented him from spilling. He drew from the glass straw, and cautiously put the delicate little glass down. Arrick had been lost in thought, sucking on his pipe, until he heard the little glass scrape onto the tiny table. He reached out and stabilized the glass for Figson, giving him an apologetic look.

"I am sorry…"

"You do not need to apologize to me, Mr. Evlan," Figson interrupted him. The older man shook his head and grunted.

"Yes, I think I do. I owe you more than silence. Here you are, wasted to a sorry state, having sacrificed your very strength and vitality…"

"But not my freedom," Figson interrupted again, his voice gravelly and hoarse. Arrick exhaled heavily and scratched his chin.

"They are alive, that is what's important. What becomes of me isn't important."

"Don't be stupid," Figson blurted. "Of course it's important. But don't speak to me of sacrifice," he went on to say. Arrick gave up and leaned back into his chair, groaning from soreness as he did.

"I am no longer a young man," he said. "No longer fit for fighting," he chuckled.

"But you won," Figson concluded. Arrick nodded.

"It has been twenty two years since I took a man's life. This time it wasn't some strange face on a battlefield, dispatched with a bayonet. This was a different thing. It was murder. Justified or no."

"Was it… difficult? Did he fight hard?" Arrick lifted his wounded arm, studying the neat stitches placed by one of his naval doctors.

"He was at the establishment belonging to Mrs. Voss," Arrick said with disdain. This was a popular hospitality house in the city. "He was staying in one of the lodging rooms up on the fourth floor. A hovel of a place that reeks of old ale and armpits," he snorted sardonically. Figson managed a wan smile.

"He opened the door without asking who it was, so arrogant. The little bottle was yanking at my hand like it wanted to punch its way through my fingers. He stood in the doorway in a state of undress. At first he looked amused and then his face melted into hatred. I'll never forget that wraith in the bottle, emitting such heat and fury, yanking my hand about. I used that momentum to punch him straight in the gob.

"He flew back onto the floor. But he recovered quickly. It was a struggle. I had a great deal of anger in me, and it felt as if the fury of the wraith somehow possessed me too, for I still cannot fathom how I gained an advantage on him, especially when I took out the knife. He turned it on me once, and got my arm. But that was all the blood I was willing to let him shed. He'd done enough damage. I buried the thing under his chin, up into his skull.

"The wraith in the vial had fallen to the floor, and the thing was rattling and flipping about like a fish on the deck. I reached for it and set the thing free. I will never forget what happened then. It was chilling. The oily thing slithered from the bottle and enveloped Eldus' body. It encased him, and allowed no means of escape for his spirit, except into its grasp. I saw the spirit leave him; I've never seen that before. The shape writhed from the body, but was suffocated by the wraith that bound it. I watched him struggle to escape the creature that wrapped around him, and I could make out the shape of his face and his hands as he fought against this membrane that the wraith had become. The wraith withdrew and took the struggling Eldus with it, fighting to escape all the while. The shadether opened for it, and they were gone. I could swear I heard the man's screams as the aperture closed."

Figson shuddered quietly underneath his pile of blankets. There was a thoughtful silence and then he spoke. "There was a haunting this last night, in the house. Your wife has vowed to leave this place with the girls."

"My grandfather paid a tidy sum to have this estate built, and he spent more finding just the right spot where there were no weak spots where the ghosts could come through," he groaned in defeat. "But that is of no import now."

"A ghoster could control it."

"Naya just fears the girls will find some way to remember what happened. We will cross that bridge when we come to it I suppose," he gusted out. Arrick then prepared his pipe for another filling. Figson was about to protest when he felt a flush of tingling warmth flood the nape of his neck, and flow pleasantly down his spine. With a smile, he looked to Arrick who arched a brow in response.

"The girls are waking," he murmured gently. "It is time for me to go." Arrick stood and put his pipe in the faceted glass dish made to receive it. He wheeled Figson out to the hall where he issued orders to have him sent home. Naya was informed that Figson sensed their awakening, and darted upstairs. Figson departed quietly, his strength slowly seeping back as steadily as the girls regained awareness.

Dae felt bed sore. She was astonished to find herself in her bed at all. Last she remembered she was with Renna, walking the falls and searching for some new blackberries. She was astonished to see a stranger tending to her, lifting her hands and washing them with a rag dampened with warm water.

"Who are you?" she asked.

"I am Eeda, I am your nurse. You and your sister have taken very ill. You have both survived the Avasanne but you are weakened from so many weeks in bed. Don't try to move suddenly."

"Where is Lexa?"

"If you mean your abigail, she is no longer employed here," the woman replied. Dae was disoriented and confused. At that moment her mother entered the room and threw herself onto Dae, showering her with kisses and embracing her. Dae, weak and still mystified returned her mother's embraces and wiped away her joyous tears.

"Why is Lexa gone mother?"

"You both were so ill, several of the servants refused to provide care, so I had to let them go," she replied. "But you and Renna, you are better now. Renna is waking as well. I am so glad to see you both better," she exclaimed. Dae leaned back in her bed, her face awash with bemusement. She remembered nothing of being ill; of becoming ill. It was all too strange. So many weeks lost, she discovered, to a restless unconsciousness, to fever and thrashing while the disease possessed her and her sister. She was glad to see her mother, and soon after, her father, both looking so very happy and relieved.

For several days, the girls were given very little chance to leave their rooms. There was the work of gaining strength, of eating and fattening their wasted bodies, of learning to stand and walk without the weakened muscles giving way. But at length they were given chairs in which they could be rolled about in, so they could sit in the conservatory and enjoy the morning sun, and watch the gardener tend to the hothouse plants and greenery. They could sit out on the patio outside the drawing room and take the autumn warmth. They could soon walk in small measures through the rose garden and pick fruit from the orchard. It was a process to endure, but in a few weeks, the girls were nearing their normal lives. They could not yet explore the steep paths to the falls, for they still became winded too quickly, but they could move about the house in soft footfalls, and enjoy the freedoms they had before they were ill.

Oddly, the circle of friends Naya had worked so hard to cultivate for the girls had evaporated. No cards were dropped at the door for visitation. No letters arrived. Their mother's silent disgust did not prompt the already introverted girls to seek their peers out. They had never cared much for the forced interactions anyway. So the time passed quietly. Dae took to the office to help her father with the business ledgers, and Renna resumed her various crafts and reading.

"Father, where has Mr. Howkes gone? I haven't seen him at all; he is usually here more often than not. It seems particularly lonely in here without him," Dae asked one morning as she and her father worked shortly after breakfast. He smirked to himself before answering.

"You know how hard Mr. Howkes has been working to secure new clients for the firm, my dear. He has other people that divide his attention these days. He'll surely come see us soon," Arrick replied. Dae offered her father a soft smile and continued adding numbers from the shuffle of documents into the neat ledger. The work had suffered during their ostensible illness, and there was much to catch up on. It kept them both busy. Arrick rarely worked outside of the home now that the girls had returned.

The following day, a Mr. Lemmes from the shipping concern came by with some permit documents that required signatures. He was let in by the new footman, and he was led to the drawing room to wait for Mr. Evlan to meet him. As they passed the parlor, he heard music, and chanced to peer through the partly opened door to see Miss Renna Evlan seated in the light of the tall window, playing on the piano. Wan and stunned, he met Mr. Evlan and acquired the signatures he needed, and left the house with gossip to share.

News of Renna being alive spread quickly from the immediate businesses belonging to Mr. Evlan to the closed society of the city's upper crust. Rumours and speculation were rampant, and it began to climb the ranks. The word resurrection was never overtly spoken, but it didn't have to be. It took only two and a half days for the rumour mill to reach the ministry of the spectral arts, and another few hours to reach the ears of the royal crown.

Dae was sitting in the parlor working on some paper scrolling with her sister when the servant brought her a card. She read the name on it. Mr. Hevram Mazell, EthMn Gh Esq, DoSA. "He's here to see father?"

"I believe so," the servant replied. Dae shrugged.

"Bring him in here, I'll let him know father is at the warehouses today," she said. The footman nodded and went to fetch the visitor.

The footman returned with the visitor in tow, and he left him when he passed through the door. Dae rose, as did Renna, and she curtseyed along with her sister in greeting. The gentleman, a tall, leggy fellow in all black save for white stockings, bowed deeply in return, studying each girl in turn. Dae extended her arm. He took her hand in his, enveloping it up to her wrist with his long fingers. His grip was quite tight, almost painful. He released it and gazed for a moment at her elegant, finely shaped fingers and wrist. She found that off-putting, and pulled her fingers out of his grasp, hiding her arm behind her back. She shifted uncomfortably.

"I'm sorry Mr. Mazell, my father is at the warehouses at port this afternoon. I shall however, pass on your card."

"Indeed, how kind of you my dear," he replied in a nasal voice. "I understand you and your fair sister have recently recovered from a cruel illness. I am glad to hear you are both well now."

"Why thank you, sir," Renna replied politely.

"Let your father know we will be visiting him again soon." The man then bowed again and exited the room, showing himself the way out.

"Ugh," Renna exclaimed under her breath, flopping back into her chair. "What a slithery looking character," she murmured. Dae could not disagree. She put his card on the table and sat down again, unconsciously rubbing her wrist where he had squeezed her so tightly.

The next day, Mr. Mazell returned with a pair of heavy-set looking gentlemen in his company. Mr. Evlan impassively greeted them. After a bit of time locked in the office with the trio, Arrick left with them without a word. A few hours later, Figson arrived with a look of worry across his face. He was just in the parlor with the family when Mr. Mazell and his henchmen came for Mrs. Evlan. With that, he handed Figson a document of arrest, and took the stoic Naya with them, leaving Dae, Renna and Figson alone to figure it all out for themselves.

MIRANDA MAYER

BOOK 3
THE PROBLEM OF LIVING

The memory of the shadether was a bleak and horrid one for Dae. Being conscious of the life thief, and feeling her essence being consumed; these recovered moments were best left forgotten. In the ethers, they were alone and terrified. The trauma of it clung to her, but she was grateful that Renna would be spared this knowledge. But what hung heaviest on her heart now were the clear memories of Figson. And how out of step they were with the person she was now. She did not know what to feel. She now remembered his accompanying her to the cotillion, and how it made her feel. She had always felt it, especially after the incident with the Kallenback man, but her memories had been curtailed after then, and her familiar affection for Figson remained passive, for she had no memory of it blooming into something greater. Or perhaps no memory of her realizing it was something greater all along. She felt absolutely horrid.

Lady Aylange had seen her through it. She hand held her hands and daubed her tear-soaked face with her soft kerchief, her velvety voice low and soothing. She now sat next to Dae, her arm wrapped around her shoulders, holding her close. She smelled lovely, her perfume a delicate rose scent. "My dearest girl, you poor thing," she murmured. The Lady had a deep, melodious voice, with a smooth, calming power to it. She was a stunning creature. A member of an ancient line of nobility, she had a patrician air about her. Her clothing was tasteful and rich, not too overdone, a combination of sheer gauzy silks lying over an under gown of powdery muslin. Her gown was a striking vibrant blue, the pastel beneath softening it, and giving it a sinuous movement. She had a long train on the back, and she wore slippers red as cherries, with a sash under her bust the same tone, that was tied in a bow on the high back, which tumbled in ribbons down the densely pleated skirts.

Her hair was golden, swept up onto the back of her head into a pile of handsome curls decorated with a garland of pearls. She was sweetly familiar to Amdreus when they arrived. He was surprised how quickly she had accepted their request for a meeting. Dae, swept up into Ammette's coach with Figson, the Magister and Amdreus; still shaken from the attack of the ghost of Mr. Eldus Kabe, was unprepared for what was to come.

Lady Aylange received them in a cavernous sitting room facing the west, where the afternoon sun cast itself through the windows in veils of gold, catching the motes and setting them afire. Lady Aylange was arranged like the figure of a portrait, seated serenely on a settee in the path of the light, her wheaten hair turned to gold by the sunlight. She stood when they were ushered in by the butler, and reached out both of her arms to Amdreus, with a whimsical tilt of her head and a beaming smile. She was absolutely a vision of beauty.

"Amdreus, you silly man, why have you not come to see me? It's been an age," she intoned, her sensuous voice like music. Mr. Drouwd bowed easily and then embraced her, kissing both of her hands.

"My Lady," he replied. "You are well aware of my current state. I am no longer disposed to grace the fine parlors of the titled and the rich. I am but a humble ghoster now." She laughed and waved her hand dismissively at him.

"As if I would ever bow to such conventions. You are my cousin, my dear, how could I think to abandon you? Come, sit down," she waved her arm to the chair. "Tell me who these fine people are, my dear," she added. Amdreus turned to Figson, and introduced him.

"This is Mr. Howkes. He is the attorney for the Evlan family, and has been responsible for the oversight and care of the two girls after their parents were charged and arrested by the crown," he explained, sitting down. The Lady curtseyed elegantly to Figson, who returned the greeting with a stiff, nervous bow. "This is a court Magister here to depose the girls. Mr. Lesk, I believe." The handsome man bowed for the lady with a sweeping, confident air. His politeness was reciprocated by her ladyship, and she invited him to sit. She then turned to look at Dae, and her eyes brightened.

"Oh, I see…" she said. "I know now to what we owe the honor of this visit," she declared. "A beautiful little revenant. Do come here, girl, let me see you up close," she said. Dae flushed and stepped forward, curtsying.

"I am Dae Evlan, my Lady."

"Indeed you are. Here, let me take your hand," the lady reached for it, her pale skin almost the same value as Dae's. She turned her hand up, and examined the delicate skin of the wrist, and then studied Dae's face almost uncomfortably closely. "Remarkable," she breathed. "One of the finest revenants I've ever seen," she declared. "I don't mean to objectify you, my dear child, but one artist must acknowledge the good work of another. You understand," she said. Dae smiled good-humouredly and nodded.

"Now do sit, sweet thing, and let us have a conversation. I have no other engagements today, so I am all yours. Do allow me to furnish everyone with some refreshment first. I could use a nice cup of tea, and usually, with searches, the revenant will require a bracing cup of tea too when this is all over." She said this with a touch of foreboding.

Dae wasn't sure what Lady Aylange was, in the category of those with death-related magical abilities. She'd never heard of a searcher, but that is what Amdreus described her as in the coach to her house. Figson seemed also ignorant of this type of person, and seemed to foster trepidation about what she could reveal to Dae.

"Does she read the person and tell what she sees? For how can one be sure they speak the truth?" he said in an irritated tone, his arms crossed. Amdreus furrowed his brow and looked at him in puzzlement.

"It doesn't work that way. The memories are returned to the revenant," he retorted. Dae frowned.

"What if the truth is too difficult for her to bear? Have you thought of that? What if the truth hurts her more than it is worth? Her haunting ghost has been trapped. The Magister has him for the court; that is all that is required."

"Will it free papa?" Dae asked Figson. He stopped talking and pursed his lips.

"Possibly. If it can be proved that the deathwitch acted independently of your parents."

"But they did not report you," the Magister grunted, "and this provides the opportunity to know the whole truth."

"If Miss Evlan chooses to share it," Amdreus interjected. "The searcher has her vow of confidence, she cannot be compelled to speak of anything she might learn from her exchange with Miss Evlan. Keep that in mind, Magister. This is *her* truth first."

"It would be considered contempt of court to willfully withhold relevant information derived from…"

"Hearsay, it's all hearsay!" barked Figson. "You have no way of proving anything based on recovered memories, Magister. Do not try to intimidate Miss Evlan. She will decide what to share. Her good conscience will guide her testimony."

"The ministry of the death arts has stringent protections for the memories of revenants; it's antiquated law, but it exists," Amdreus added. "Contempt of court will not stand on this I'm afraid. Besides, this is only if the lady can glean anything at all. It's never a certainty." They fell silent after that.

Figson's thoughts remained fast on the ghost in Amdreus' possession. If they wanted to question it, the court could bring in a ghoster. And they could, given the apparition's cooperation, discover that he was perhaps the murderer, but he was not the resurrectionist. Whether or not this ghoster would believe him was the question, and he would surely implicate Figson given the chance to communicate from the ethers. He had never even thought to consider that the determined vengeful person would continue to carry on his campaign to inflict pain on Figson into the afterlife. How he even escaped the clutch of the life thief, to become a full on ghost able to cross to the living world, that was beyond him. Eldus was a manipulative, sneaky cur even in death.

What he did know is that the appearance of that ghost meant that he must resign himself to his fate. His priorities remained Dae and Renna. To get the magister away from the girls was his first concern. He knew, with Eldus' vengeful desire to hurt Figson, it was only a matter of time before the sword fell. Making sure that happened back in Garvash was his priority. If there were going to be consequences for his part in everything, he wanted the girls to be far away from them. If only, thought he, had the magister not stopped the ghoster in time. If only Amdreus had squeezed Eldus into oblivion like he had done so easily with that little shade. He emitted a sigh.

Now, Dae would remember everything that occurred to her in the weeks prior to her death. What would she think of him now? She would remember his presence in the ethers, when he tore her from death, and she would recall being forced back into her token, and being reabsorbed into a body that looked like her, but belonged to nobody. To leave this place was his only desire. To leave and take his tragedy with him, along with the magister and the hateful ghost of the man who ruined so many lives; all because he despised Figson.

Dae did recall everything now, but she processed it in her unique way, as she had when she was told she had died. She sat with the lady in solitude, drinking from a tulip shaped glass a fragrant sherry. Her mind was still buzzing from the lady's presence within it, as she walked with Dae through her closed memories and helped her sort them out. Her tears had dried. And now they worked through the information, piecing what they could together from the fragments of events and interactions, from the forced possession and engagement with Eldus, to Figson's declaration and her joyful response. The air of elation they shared before she and Renna were cut down by the invasion of their bodies. She remembered being pulled through the ethers with Renna, trying to reach for her but having no arms. Flailing and terrified in the ethers, wrapping herself around Renna's shrinking being as the countless dead surrounded them.

Her skin was cold. The lady's hand fell upon her arm, so warm and alive and real. "Do not let the memories frighten you, dear. Death is natural, and when it is your time it will not be like it was this time. Your passing was anything but natural."

"Figson. He revived us. Father knew. They were there, both mother and father," she whispered. "They are guilty in the eyes of the law. I cannot save them. I hoped *some* truth would be revealed that could save them. Now poor Figson will pay too. He did it for me. He sacrificed everything for us. They all did. Father hoped to free Figson so he could protect me."

"My dear, it changes little. That was then. Your life is different now. Your choices are different. And the choices made by Figson and your parents were knowingly made. The risk was willingly taken."

"Yes," she muttered. The lady took her hand and squeezed it.

"There's a reason there are few of us in this world, Dae. The nascent Revenant is not meant to know the why. It is meant to simply accept the chance it has been given to live the life it has. Figson loved you enough to give you that gift. Honor his sacrifice by cherishing it." Dae nodded, tight lipped. With a sigh, she stood.

"I thank you Lady Aylange," she curtsied. "I will return to the others now." She bustled past the searcher, and went back to the room where the rest remained, in silent patience. When she entered the room, her eyes found Figson's, and she gave him a lingering glance before exclaiming that it was time to go.

The magister pressed her for information all through the five hours in the coach. Dae offered little. "I am not sure what I saw,

Magister. So much must have happened outside of my presence. My memories are blurred by the invasive consciousness inside me. Even the lady could barely make anything of it. I saw Eldus. I saw him force a spirit to possess me; to make me form a contract of promise with him. I witnessed the invasion of the life thieves, one after the other. My spirit so aware while my body fell. I became very ill, and the presence of those things made everything unclear. I do not recall anything of my resurrection," she lied. "Only waking up and being told I was beset by the Avasanne," she insisted for what felt like the thousandth time. Dae's composure was fraying, and she remained silent after that. Amdreus doted upon her, calming her with quiet words, and reading to her.

The return to Fallswell was a relief. But the feeling of calm did not remain for long. The first moment Dae had alone, she sent a note to Figson to meet her in the library. Her stomach roiling, she waited for him. He did arrive at length, looking quite uncomfortable the moment he set foot into the room. He closed the door behind him, and bowed shallowly to her. She took in his dark clothes, his pale face, his stringy hair.

"I will not lie to you, Mr. H…" She paused. "Figson," she said quietly. "I have been thrown into the greatest state of confusion. And as much as I would like to address how divided I feel in my heart about all these romantic matters, I can think only of two things. Two things that preoccupy my mind so greatly I can scarce breathe. How can we save you, and how can we save my parents. That vengeful ghost in Amdreus' pocket will destroy all hope of that. He must be removed from the quotient if anything can happen to spare you and my parents," she said in desperation. Figson found himself unexpectedly relieved by her words. He slid into a chair and folded his hands on the table.

"What would the destruction of the ghost achieve, objectively? Aside from raising more suspicion? The act would prevent me from being identified as the deathwitch; but it would not help your father. And the fact that your mother was arrested shows how little tolerance the crown has, for your mother had no hand in any of it except to be present. They charged her for not reporting the crime she had knowledge of. I am your resurrector. How long can I hope to escape that crime? And how can I sit by and hope to, when your father and mother are hung for it?"

"Then what?" Dae blurted. "Then you must flee! The magister knows of the ghost yes, but you can simply leave; vanish into the islands, or onto the west mainlands!" she whispered desperately. A small ghost flitted through the room as she spoke, tipping over an empty vase on the sill. She stood and righted the object, her eyes focusing on something out the window.

"Once I have been identified, and the magister has confirmed my escape, I will have to be consigned to a lifetime of flight, Dae. It is not a life I wish to lead. I am prepared to face the consequences, especially if it means it will offer you and your sister a clean start; and possibly a new start for your parents. I am the closure the court requires for this all to conclude and for life to move on," he replied in a soft voice.

"Tell me what we must do. Tell me and I will do it," she turned to face him and cried. Figson sighed loudly and shook his head slowly, pressing his fingers into his eyes and then drawing them out to pinch the bridge of his ungainly nose.

"Your parents will hang, Dae. The only recourse is to do what I have done. Bring them back. Do it here, where such acts are not so scrutinized. Where they are unknown. They lost everything anyway. They can begin again. I have no doubt your kind aunt would be delighted to help them." She stared at him with wide, disbelieving eyes.

"Break the law again?"

"You needn't do a thing. I could arrange it. I have connections." She blinked in incredulity and stepped back, turning her back to him, her hands wringing before her. "It means I would return to Garvash. Make arrangements as expeditiously as I can before the ghost tells his tale."

"Then what?" she snapped.

"As they say, I pay the proverbial piper."

"Don't be stupid, Figson. You must not surrender yourself," she retorted, her eyes glistening.

"I would not risk your wellbeing by dispatching with the spectral witness, Miss Evlan. That is that. If you and Renna are to remain on the legal register as innocent products of a crime, the last thing we should do is destroy the ghost. That would immediately involve you in it. For in doing so, it would mean that you withheld relevant knowledge from the crown about the case. I will not do it. And please do not ask Mr. Drouwd to compromise his integrity either. He loves you already, I can see it. He would do it to help you. But I beg you not to involve him like that."

Dae's eyes fell. Then she looked up again. "What of you? Can we not resurrect you?" Her features brightened and she smiled.

"I would rather not, Dae." He said this with finality, and stood. "This is not subject for debate. If I die, I shall remain dead," he grunted. He unfolded himself from his seat and rose to his feet, his eyes resting regretfully upon her. He gave her a shallow bow and exited. Dae waited until he was well outside of earshot before she succumbed to helpless tears.

Amdreus was displeased with Dae when she told him she would accompany the duo back to Garvash to witness the trial and sentencing of her parents. He stood with his back to her, staring gravely into the fire, one hand braced on the mantel, the other in a fist on his hip. "I don't think it's a good idea, Miss Evlan," he muttered quietly. The rest of the family and party were across the formal parlor. Renna was chatting easily with Figson, and Ammette and Mr. Lesk were playing a game of Highwayman. It was shortly after dinner. Hatter was at Dae's feet. Although he had missed his master, he seemed determined to absorb Dae's company as well.

"I know all that you know. Perhaps not to the extent that you do, but I know the essentials. I've been chatting with your ghost," he mumbled. Dae said nothing. She could only suspire in defeat. The ghosts of Fallswell had been unusually still and quiet since the incident with Eldus. The ghoster destroying one of their kind had instilled a proper respect for the man, and when he was in the house, which was more often than not, these days, the spirits kept to themselves. All except Ortner, who refused to leave Ammette's side or the top of her head.

Dae was unaccustomed to such quiet in the house, and almost felt like she missed it. Or perhaps she missed the time before everything was upset by the arrival of Figson and the Magistrate, and that of Eldus Kabe's ghost. Now, because of it all, she would have to leave Fallswell and face the reality of her parents' trial. She had no choice.

"Figson has chosen to surrender to the authorities," she told Amdreus in a low voice. "He will do it after they have a spectral ghoster interrogate Eldus. He will gladly indict Figson. According to him, he and Eldus shared an inexplicable rivalry, and this Eldus has been so bent on hurting Figson…"

"Yes. I saw the events unfold from his point of view when I explored the ghost's collected memories."

"You interrogated him?"

"I read him. Without his consent. But I don't care about a dead murderer's consent." She chuffed at his words, and shook her head in disbelief.

"I wanted to understand why you were so upset after speaking to my cousin. I am sorry," he grumbled. "It was presumptuous of me. But your confusion and hurt were of such depth, all the way home. I… I had to understand."

Dae should have been upset. He had invaded the privacy of her past, using a hateful spirit to do so. But she could not dismiss his concern and his worry. She pretended to be more taken aback than she truly was.

"Never fear. I learned more about him and your attorney than I did about you. But I did learn something crucial. That Howkes loves you." She lowered her eyes to her hands and smoothed out her skirts.

"I learned that as well, when I spoke to your cousin." Amdreus nodded and lowered himself into the chair angled towards hers, leaning in to speak privately. "It is his love that brought all this upon you."

She nodded again. He pressed on. "Eldus spent his entire life wrapped up in hatred and jealousy of anyone of greater skill and intelligence as he. It began with a brother who was like your friend. Awkward but brilliant. He detested him for how easily brilliance and talent came to him. He both loved and hated his brother. And when his rash and irresponsible nature caused him to lose his place as eldest heir to his brother, he nearly beat him to death in a rage. His father had him disinherited completely, and chased away. He met Figson shortly after.

"Figson has always acted with integrity. And his hard work and determination earned him all the distinctions that this Kabe fellow wanted but did not care to work for. He used people to increase his grades at university, he indebted himself to so many so he could maintain the image of a titled heir, and live as such. He dabbled in deathwitch work so he could finance himself through school. He worked illegally performing all sorts of questionable acts. Possessions for gain, partial resurrections for the black market of limbs. He was not a good man. He had aspirations. The firm for which Figson worked was the same that handled his family's affairs. He was determined to show his father up by availing himself to their legal matters, and influencing them for the worse. He had from the moment he was ejected from his home, striven to become an attorney there. But he wasn't good enough. Even cheating his way through, he couldn't make muster.

"Imagine his rage when your friend Figson was asked by the partners themselves to join the firm. Oh, that rage boils still red hot in that spirit even now. Figson was his bane. Showing him up again and again, better at everything, even deathwitchery. Then he saw you." Amdreus stopped and looked up from his far off stare, gazing at Dae. "He witnessed how Figson adored you. How he beamed when you were nearby. He knew that he cherished you, and all he wanted to do from that moment was to destroy that for Figson. At whatever cost." Dae blanched.

"You were rich; he was destitute, living on borrowed money, with debtors at his heels. He spent the money earned at his firm irresponsibly. He did not care; for all he ever lived for was to spite those that he believed hurt him. He saw you as a double prize. A rich woman to make him easy, and the priceless gift, the woman adored by his most despised rival. He was going to win you using whatever means he could.

"He did what he did to hurt the lawyer. Your father took his life. But it was no great inconvenience for the man, for he was free of the debts and responsibility. Oh, but Figson's final assault upon his victory was to steal you back from death. Oh, that enraged his spirit. He was utterly consumed by so much hatred he drew the bleakest souls like moths to a flame, and absorbed their strength to give him power in this world. He was determined to take you from

Figson in any way he could. He would not have Figson know any happiness anymore."

"But I went out and found you," Dae whispered. He smiled, and so did she. There was a loaded silence as they basked in it.

"Do you think I am … distasteful. Because I am a Revenant?" she suddenly asked. He gave her a look of ridicule and laughed.

"I think you are resplendent, Miss Dae." She flushed, and looked down at her fingers. She could not deny the swell of affection for him. She had loved Figson in such a different way. It was a sweet, accepting kind of affection. But Amdreus, he stirred up such passions and feelings she had never felt before. Even in the thick of all this awfulness, he made her ears and cheeks warm with regard.

They sat in silence enjoying the company of the other for a moment. Then he spoke again as if decided upon something. "I will be accompanying you to Garvash then," he declared. "I do not trust the crown to be careful with the ghost, and there is risk that he could harm you again. I will retain custody of the ghost until it is time to destroy him." Dae offered him a sweet smile, and nodded.

Across the room, Figson observed them. Dae's colored cheeks and soft smiles were all he could see. With a sigh of resignation, he turned his attention back to the affable and chatty Renna, envying her for her innocence of everything. It didn't matter in the long run anyway.

Dae had hoped that if she were to subject herself to a ship again in her life, it would be to return to her home. That the throne would have cleared her parents of wrongdoing, and returned her father's assets. But this was not the case. It was a return to bid them farewell. Renna had insisted upon going as well, and Dae knew that as much as she hoped to protect her younger sibling from the reality of what was happening, she would have to let Renna stand on her own feet. However in the end she discouraged Renna from going. Sulking, Renna did not see her sister off, and remained locked in her room weeping. Ammette sent the party off with a hamper of comforts, and made them promise to return as soon as they could.

****

Being aboard ship with both Figson and Amdreus was a challenge for Dae. It was evident to both young men that she was divided by her opposing feelings, and each day in Figson's company made it more difficult for her. She made an overt effort to remain impassive and focus on the important matter; but Amdreus felt the effect of the secretive bond the attorney had with Dae. He found them often in the small common space below decks, huddled together, talking. He suspected Figson had a plan to resurrect the Evlans. He didn't like that they did not include him in this plan if that was indeed the case.

He was now privy to the secret that Figson was the one to resurrect the sisters, and he was well aware that Figson's fate rested on the struggling bottle in his pocket. Dae had not asked him to help; to release the specter or destroy it. Amdreus could only fix his confidence on the notion that Dae was earnest at least in her blushes and smiles and that regardless of the outcome for Figson and her parents, he would be returning to Mahalav with the Revenant he had come to love. He knew his role would be a supportive one for the months to come. And he held onto that promise regardless of what happened between now and then.

As days wore by, the silence also wore on Amdreus. The complicity between Dae and the attorney appeared to be certain and Amdreus began to worry for Dae. He took a moment to confront Figson when he found him alone.

"How could you allow her to risk herself, Howkes? To become involved in a resurrection?" Amdreus was direct, his whisper harsh and forceful. Figson, who had been standing in deck staring at the isle of Havettem as it glided by, was startled by Amdreus. He tore his eyes from the bristling spires of the Aydet temple that consumed the towering ochre cliffs on the western peninsula, and spread like a crawling vine along the edge of the slab of an island. The bay was at high tide, and it looked like a garden of pale exotic blossoms; the sails of ships unfurling in a bouquet of petals. Orchids on the sea. Smoke rose up from myriad chimney stacks from the city, the pillars slanting east with the present wind. It was an astonishing sight.

"I wonder why all the houses on Havettem are all painted that shade of ivory," Figson mused. "I've passed this isle so many times, and asked myself that question, yet have never bothered to take to port and find out for myself. It's such an impressive sight from afar. All those white faces peering out over the cliffs, the temple virtually eating up the peninsula. So many towers…" he mumbled.

"The Havetti people believe in natural forces being influenced by aesthetics. White houses mean being respectful for the distinction between people and nature. That is what I was told, but I suspect it's the massive deposit of gypsum they have on the southern end of the island." Amdreus' furor had been deflated instantly by Figson's detached, almost indifferent air. He stared at the unfortunate fellow, passing again through his mind all that the ghost had revealed. He wished he could know the whole story from an unbiased point of view. The ghost of Eldus Kabe was anything but unbiased when it came to his hatred for Figson Howkes. Amdreus looked at the plain fellow, a few years older than he, his face filled with a sorrowful resignation; but he could not truly grasp what it was that had made Eldus hate him so.

Figson's faraway gaze seemed to retract into awareness, and he turned, leaning on the ship's railing next to Amdreus, crossing his arms. "I know you do not know me well, Drouwd, but I wish to ask something of you. I hope you will listen before you respond." Amdreus nodded, watching for sign of Dae or the Magister.

"Once Dae has seen her parents, I beg you take her away. Do not let her witness their execution."

"I will try."

"It could well be my execution too, depending on how much that abomination you are toting about with you cooperates. I suspect if it is to indict me, ghostly Eldus will be a model witness."

"I hardly think there won't be reasonable doubt considering what a monster he has already been proven to be."

"Dae is with us. They need only have the ghoster examine her hidden markings. I carry the same ones," he put his hand on his forearm. Always hidden beneath his shirtsleeves were the brands of a deathwitch. They were there at birth, and remained. It was a birthmark in a distinctive figure. They were passed on from one generation to the next. Figson's great grandmother had possessed this symbol until she died. It was already on his arm when he was born. But it was sometimes known to appear on young people too, after the passing of their deathwitch relative.

Ghosters were different on that end. They were born with the second voice and the etherforce. It was natural to them as breathing. Deathwitches had to learn. They had to perform rites and rituals to tap into powers that ghosters possessed naturally. They required elements and substances to connect them to the power of the shadethers. Deathwitchery was a powerful skill, but it took a greater tax on its bearers and required additional knowledge to perform.

"I could drop the bastard right into the sea you know," Amdreus blurted.

"It would prevent nothing for the Evlans."

"Yes, but it would save you."

"It would cast suspicion on Dae," he snapped. There was a pall. "They are innocent both. It was a conscious choice, Drouwd. We all knew the risk. Their deaths had been made public before it was even considered to revive them. Their reappearance was not discreet. We were reckless. We were desperate with grief." Figson exclaimed this with a passionate furor, his eyes burning with resolve.

"I can try to fix this for her. I have contacts. I can make this right. But Dae thinks she can save me. She must let me go, and do what is best. Take the relics we can get from her parents and go back to Mahalav. My mother can send you a deathwitch willing to do the job. Finding their spirits from such a distance will make it difficult for the deathwitch, but it can be done. Just please, get her off of Garvash as soon as the trial ends. I beg you." Amdreus nodded.

"If it should come to your being convicted, and subsequently," he paused, uncomfortable; "that you should be executed, then can we not simply do the same? If the risk is to be taken for mother and father Evlan, why not you too?"

"Deathwitches cannot be resurrected. Our power upon the death of our bodies, returns to the shadethers until our mark is passed on to the next generation, and our spirits are bound to the ethers because of what we are. If we are resurrected, we are only a facsimile of what we once were. True abominations."

"I did not know that." Amdreus was earnest in his bewilderment. There was still so much he did not know about the death arts. He frowned in thought.

"It is not commonly known, it is a deathwitch secret. It is speculated that the powers of the shadethers most likely wanted to prevent deathwitches from saving only their own," Figson explained.

"There is no way one can recapture the powers and the mark of power before it takes hold of its heir?" Amdreus asked. Figson's brow rose over his left eye and lips twisted in thought. "Like the Echinn do when their shaman pass their powers onto their apprentices. They've been known to even take them away from others, have they not?"

"To what end? I would still be a misshapen, monstrous freak if someone brought me back. Powers or no, that is no life." Amdreus nodded, realizing his ignorance. He understood, with some measure of sorrow, that for Figson, a life without the regard of Dae could not be borne by this man so much in love. He saw a resignation in Figson. An acceptance of what was to come.

There was a moment of silence as they both contemplated this truth, and then Amdreus resolved to do as Figson asked.

"I will respect your wishes. Does the lady Dae know that you cannot return?"

"I have told her that it is impossible for me to be resurrected." Amdreus frowned. "She might think I am self-sacrificing. I am not. If I could be selfish enough to ask someone to commit a crime to return me to this world, I would. I will not lie to you. I love her. I have always loved her." Amdreus felt a chill when he said this. "I cannot say I am not made jealous by the way she looks at you, and the way she speaks to you. But I also am comforted in knowing that she has someone to lean on when things are difficult. And I am impressed by the fact that you do not frown on her for being what she is."

"A revenant?"

"Yes."

"She is nothing less than what she was before she perished. She is merely in a newer body." Amdreus shrugged.

"She is more than just the sum of what you see. She is brilliant, and clever. Beautiful and wise. She has always been kind and accepting beyond anyone I've ever known in her station in life. She has a strength that would surprise you."

"I think not. I see it. I saw it in how she took everything in stride, no matter how grave her story is, she bore it like nobody I've ever known. And all she worries about is making sure her younger sister is protected from the pain of the truth."

"Do you love her?" Figson asked. Amdreus smiled sadly at Figson, whose eyes were filled with hurt and sorrow.

"I think I, like you, loved her from the moment I saw her. She stood in my doorway, with the sun cast upon the fur hood around her face, those freckles across her nose, the brightness of her eyes, and the depth of her past speaking through them. I could see the aura of the shades emanating from her. It bled from her movements like a wake, leaving a mist behind. I never saw anything so graceful and lovely. She took no offense in my state of undress, and she was so businesslike. I confess I am a bit of a boor sometimes, and I imparted to her that she was a revenant in a graceless way. She took the revelation with such fortitude. How could I not be impressed? How could I not become smitten?" Figson watched Amdreus' face light up as he spoke of her, and he chewed his mandibles.

"You will promise to care for her, Amdreus. You will promise or I will haunt you with a vengeance," Figson choked. Amdreus reached up and put his hand on his new friend's shoulder, and gave him an assuring gaze.

"It's more likely she will take care of me," he said.

"Good. Then let us get this business taken care of. Then you can take her and the tokens from her parents back to Fallswell and have her be done with this whole thing." The men came to an agreement, shaking hands on it.

Dae found Figson and Amdreus together on the deck of the ship, and she wondered how these two men had become amicable from their strained silence in such a short time. She suspected there was collusion, but she had no idea over what. She wondered as she approached them, and took in Figson's clumsy smile and caring gaze, and Amdreus' confident, almost flirtatious smile. She reached them and looked at each one in turn.

"I would ask what you were talking about, but I am almost afraid to do so," she admitted. "I was left to the company of the Magister, and I thought that it was already too much punishment to return to the trial of my parents… to be locked in that stuffy little space with that man is just too much." Figson laughed and shook his head.

"Well, I shall remedy that. Shall I read to you?" She took in his face with a long, lingering gaze, and realized how resigned he appeared. Her heart immediately hurt, for the memories that had been lost to her, now recovered, were fresh and sharp. She wanted to take his hand. To cling to his arm and tell him it would be well. But she knew it wouldn't.

They arrived at Garvash at length, the air grew warmer, and the isle nations became denser as they neared the great island. The ship took to port with the evening tide, and the passengers disembarked, the group from Fallswell among the parade of people wavering on the stone pier as they adjusted from their sea legs.

Figson had written ahead to his household, and had a coach waiting for them at the top of the pier. Dae and Amdreus were loaded in, and they were conveyed through the bustling waterfront to the center of the city, to his narrow, towering town house. There, the three of them; having left the Magister to his own devices, settled into their lodging. Dae was given a modest set of apartments on the top floor of the town house. She thanked the servant girl that led her in, and then closed the door. With a great sigh, she sank down on the edge of the bed, and started to cry.

News of their return set the process into motion; the Magister would present his evidence from the depositions and the ghost that Amdreus insisted on holding onto. Amdreus departed first thing in the morning, on summon from the courts, to bring the specter to the court for evidence. That left Dae and Figson alone together for most of the day. She joined Figson for breakfast and sat across from him at the table.

"I don't have any children or a wife, and my fortune is mine," Figson said quietly, without any preamble or greeting. "I want you to know that I wrote a will and testament last night, and I have instructed that my estate be liquidated and that the money put into investments, from which the dividends will be sent to you as support, so that your care and that of your sister would not be dependent on anyone." Dae's hands fell still, her cutlery in her fingers, and she suddenly began to weep again. Figson stood and walked 'round the table.

He knelt by her chair, and took her hands, and she turned to look at him, her eyes glassy with tears. "Do not weep, Dae. It will be well." This only made her weep harder, and she boldly leaned forward and laid her forehead on his shoulder, the tears flowing.

"What you have done and sacrificed for me Figson will never be well," she sobbed, her words made staccato by the tears. Her shoulders wracked with her sobs.

"Do not break your heart over it, Dae. It is what I wanted. It was my choice. It is because I love you, and always have."

"Oh, Figson, if only things had been different."

"I brought this fate onto you, Dae. There would have been no death, no resurrection if it weren't for Eldus. He was my problem, my demon, and his hatred should never have touched you. Or Renna. But we cannot change what is. And I will be safe in the hands of the shades, Dae. It is where my spirit belongs. It is where *I* belong." She wept more, her arms threading up around his neck. He let her cry until she was spent and beset with hiccups. He, and his soaked shoulder then retreated, so he could hide his own misery.

"Come," he said in a broken voice. "Eat something, Dae. Let us go and take a walk together. I think we should enjoy the sun for a spell. It will do us both good. And it will soothe your worried heart." She nodded, sniffling, and he handed her his kerchief from his pocket.

"Figson…" she said, but did not continue.

They were just returning from their walk when Amdreus met them. He was walking towards the entrance of the town house when he spotted them, arm in arm, strolling down the walk towards the house. He waited for them to arrive, his eyes on Dae's puffy, reddened eyes, and her white-fingered grip on Figson's arm. The news he possessed was written on his face. And Dae, seeing his expression, began to weep anew, released Figson's arm, and dashed into the house. Figson's defeated expression fell upon Amdreus like a heap of bricks, and he patted Figson's shoulder before they followed Dae into the house. Figson glanced at Amdreus.

"The ghost was loquacious, as you knew he would be. His guilt in his prior crimes was evident, but the resurrection made no sense if he had done it. His indictment of you was taken into consideration, and you will be summoned tomorrow, along with Dae to verify the symbols. It's only a matter of time. The Magister will be coming by to give you details on the matter."

"What of Eldus?" Amdreus patted his pocket.

"I thought it fitting that you be present for his destruction. It's only right. Perhaps tomorrow, after dinner. When Dae has had a little time to…" Figson nodded glumly. The two gentlemen went into the sitting room and in silence, occupied the space in quiet contemplation. The sword had fallen. It was now only a matter of awaiting the outcomes. There was little that could be done to change things now.

Dae bolted upright in her bed, sweat glistening in her brow. Something was awry. It was extremely early. The scullery maid had yet to stoke the fire. Her chest was painfully tight, and she felt the cold fingers of dread clutching her innards. She slid out of bed and pulled on her dressing gown. The darkness still lingered. Taking a candelabra from the mantel, she lit the candles. She exited her room and padded down the hall in her bare feet. There was no light emanating from the cracks underneath anyone's doors. Why she thought she would find someone awake, she was unsure. She paused at Figson's door, and put her ear to it. With a careful hand she lifted the latch and gingerly pushed the door open. It cracked silently, and she peered inside the darkened space. The bed had no occupant. It looked like it had not been slept in.

She quickly forged her way through the darkness, her candles flickering from her hurried movements. Her free hand clutched the collar of her dressing gown, and she swished down the stairs, searching. She peered into the eerily still, darkened rooms. Parlors to the dining room, no one could be found. As she passed the door to the servant's corridors, she halted. It was slightly ajar. No bustle of activity could be heard. No servants stirred. She pushed open the door and ventured into the unknown hallways, following her senses. They lured her down, to the realm of the servants. To the kitchens and basements. The hearth in the kitchen was never dark. It bellowed out its warmth with a bright orange glow that cast itself onto the spotless work table, the gleaming ceramic bowls and iron cookware; giving life to the still space. Somewhere, the strong scent of yeast bespoke of dough left to rise. She stared at the kitchen, but her instincts were left wanting. Her eyes spotted the door to the cellars, and she fixed herself on that. Pushing through the dimness with her candles, she shoved open the heavy door. And there, she came face to face with Figson Howkes' ghost.

Dae's tears had left her eyes stinging, she sat in a crumple of skirts in a scrabble of powdered elementals, seeds and grain, all poured out in a design typical of some unknown death ritual. It formed a beautiful geometric scroll design that looked like a woven blossom. Most of it was intact, except the portion that had been marred by Dae's passage, and subsequent collapse. In the center of the design was Figson's body, curled up on its side like a sleeping child, his knees drawn up to his chin. The upward arm gripped his legs. The one beneath stretched out into the design, hand unfurled, from which a black powder spilled onto the weave of elements. Empty jars and vessels were scattered about the space. Amidst the shuffle of ceramic and glass, the small round, flattened vial that had contained Eldus shone in its dull, buffed silver finish. The stopper was out, the chain that connected it snapped. The shelves of mushrooms and stored roots emitted an earthy scent that overpowered the sulfurous, stinging aroma of the various materials strewn out by Figson's careful hand.

Light pooled from the addition of more candles. First the housekeeper, then the butler, then Amdreus. Dae felt his hand fall gently on her shoulder. "The magisters are here. You should withdraw. They must make their survey." Hollow, Dae nodded. He helped her to her feet, which stung with pins and needles after sitting so long. Figson's essence, now but a little slip of a shade, remained where it had fixed itself from the moment Dae entered the root cellar. It hovered by her side. He boldly remained as she was brought up to her rooms to change. He remained as she numbly sat with the three court magisters, not hearing or listening. Hardly feeling as they grasped her arm and pressed her wrist. He hovered as she wept without restraint into Amdreus' arms after everyone had gone. Only then did she topple forward onto the floor. Feverish and in fits, she was dragged to her room.

The hall of holding was where prisoners being tried by the courts were kept for the duration of their case. It was not called a prison because the status of the occupants was still in question. There were no barred rooms, only the facility itself remained secure. It was typical of any holding hall. A moated edifice, one bridge entrance, heavily guarded. It was a construct of towering walls forming a large triangle, with sharp, lofting towers at each of the three corners. Small meurtrier windows, mere slots allowed light to pass; but little else. They peppered the outer parapet walls and the towers. The comfort or lack thereof of the chambers in which the detainees were housed was known only to their occupants.

Inside there was the bailey; a harshly angled space. One long side was occupied by an edifice that served as the administration. The other two sides had the three storied detention buildings hugging up against the deeply angled walls. The walls were made of a bleak grey stone covered in weeping stains at the corner of every window.

The windows on the inner yard were larger and the occasional pale face could be seen gazing emptily out onto the echoing yard. Dae was accompanied by Amdreus, who was there for support. Dae was weak and tremulous from her ordeal. They were led through by the Shepherd. He was a sallow, rail of a man of indeterminate age, with a hawkish nose and greasy brown hair. He had a disgusting habit of sucking in the snot in his nose, horking it up and spitting the noxious wads onto the cobbles as they walked.

Dae, already pale and frail, was forced to fight a rush of nausea every time the man did this as they crossed the yard.

She was relieved when the shepherd took them through a stuffy foyer and guided them to a room with two long sofas flanking a dark fireplace. There, he left them after directing them to sit and remain seated. There, the sallow and sickly Dae and her companion were left to ruminate while the Evlans were fetched from their chambers.

Dae's hands quivered and her breath was ragged and shallow. Her eyes caught the sight of a few ghosts lingering about the place as she had entered. Now they filtered into the room out of curiosity. Figson, although reduced to the state of a shade at present, remained with Dae. He was a new presence for his kindred spirits, and they were intrigued by him.

They danced around the two living creatures and the one small shred of ghost clinging close to them. The hall of holding had undoubtedly seen some spectral activity in its history. The shadethers were strong and ghosts were drawn to it. Dae oddly felt comforted by the presence of the spirits. There were mostly sinuous slips of black and grey, quiet and respectful, waiting it appeared as patiently as Dae and Amdreus for the arrival of the Evlans. They did not stay long, however. When the door burst open, they fled, shooting away from the guests and vanishing through the walls, leaving only the comparatively small Figson behind.

At length, the Evlans were led in. Arrick looked thin and defeated, Naya, also gaunt and drawn. She instantly burst into tears and ran to Dae, clutching onto her tightly before the guard that accompanied them intervened and parted them, sternly demanding they take their seat across from the visitors.

Dae discreetly tucked the items her mother had slipped her into the sleeve of her gown, doing so while extracting her kerchief. She daubed her eyes dry with it, and lowered herself back onto the narrow seat of the hard, flattened cushion she had been sitting on.

They had little to say except to weep. Amdreus was clumsily introduced, but after that he remained markedly silent. Arrick could only stare at the small ghost lingering at Dae's side, and occasionally mutter that Figson was a good and honorable young man. He asked if Figson's family had been informed of his death, and Dae nodded. "I sent a letter last night. They will surely have it this morning," she muttered. "Mrs. Howkes will be so distraught." She blinked, and a tear dropped into her cheek. She reached up and wiped it away with the soft muslin and lace kerchief. They spoke softly, for the guard stood by the door, watching them.

"Figson's confession did nothing to reduce the charges," Amdreus concluded during an agonizing span of silence. He spoke of the letter Figson had slid under Dae's door before he took his own life. Dae had stepped right over it when she went looking for him. It was only discovered later that morning by a servant, while Dae languished in her bed, made physically ill by her grief. The letter had been brief.

To whom it may concern,

I offer my confession of guilt in the resurrection of both Miss Dae Evlan and her sister, Renna Evlan. I must take ownership of my choices. The events occurred solely due to my troubled relationship with Eldus Kabe. My problems never should have touched this family. I persuaded Mr. Evlan to let me take the necessary tokens to return his daughters to him. I felt I owed the family this after what I brought onto them. Mrs. Evlan is innocent of all this. I used a father's grief to achieve my selfish ends, and now a whole family pays for it. I have decided to act in the only way I know how to rectify this, and hope the court will take pity on the parents of these girls. This family has known too much tragedy because of me.

Figson Howkes.

"The courts have not made any determinations on the confession, although the warden called it a 'pat and trite development'. I found that troubling." Arrick replied. "We will know when we receive the final judgment and sentencing. The crown does however take fault for the truth being revealed to you. It was not well handled by the magister, and neither of you girls should be here. Your innocence should have been protected."

"It might have been so, if Eldus hadn't been so determined to find me when he knew Figson was coming to us. Such hatred... I cannot even begin to grasp the depth of it."

"What of that thing? Is it gone yet? That despicable excuse of a ghost."

"I wanted Figson to be present when I dispatched it. But he took it from my room the night of his..." Amdreus paused, and glanced sidelong at Dae, whose pale, fragile being appeared to shudder. He sighed and resumed. "I found the vial near Figson. It was opened and emptied of its contents near his body. I saw no trace of his ghost anywhere. I suspect it must have slipped away. If it gives Dae trouble, I shall destroy it."

"I can't think of why he would set that thing free. Perhaps he destroyed it."

"Deathwitches are not skilled for ghost-killing," Amdreus said. "I can only hope he did something however, to end the thing's existence."

"Indeed. For nothing deserves more to die than that animal. I hope he made him suffer," Arrick snarled in the direction of Dae's silent misty companion. It rippled. Naya was silent all the while, seated so her body leaned on the arm of the sofa, her finger nervously working her lower lip. Her eyes were sunken and she seemed to be struggling to remain present and focused.

"You look unwell, Dae."

"I took ill after Figson died," she replied in a broken voice. "I am getting better," she assured her mother. Naya did not appear convinced.

"Renn, she is not aware of all this?"

"She knows she is a Revenant. She knows you and father are being tried for it. She knows little else." Naya nodded stiffly and chewed her nail.

"Leave, Dae. Do not stay for the conviction. It is likely weeks away still, in spite of the prosecution having obtained what it wanted." Arrick suddenly said.

"They may yet absolve you. Figson..."

"Poor fellow; never should have asked him to do it. Nobody cared more for you, Dae. He worked so hard to be worthy of you. I could have found a deathwitch who wasn't dear to us. Who wasn't family. Who could have vanished without a trace. He never left. He never left you knowing full well he could be caught. He loved you so well, he threw his life away."

"He always was worthy…" Dae whispered partly to herself, her throat tightening. Her eyes dropped. A tendril of mist brushed the top of her hand. She looked up at the apparition at her side, and began to weep anew.

"Leave. Go back to Aunt Ammette. To Renna. There is no reason for you to stay." Naya said it this time. "You can learn the outcome through the firm. They continue to defend us."

"Then I came here for nothing except to have a hand in dooming Figson." Amdreus reached boldly out and took Dae's hand.

"Figson asked me to ensure that you do not remain. You can make your goodbyes, which might still be unnecessary. Then we can go. The attorneys that Figson spoke of will manage the liquidation of his estate and see to the funds being managed. Let us go."

Dae frowned. "Your time is almost expired," the guard blurted loudly from the doorway. The four of them looked at the large man, and then back at one another.

"Promise me you will leave as soon as possible." Dae nodded weakly.

"Would that I could embrace you both," she sighed. The guardian decided they were done, and approached, gesturing for the Evlans to stand. They complied. He grasped the each by the lower arm and guided them out. Neither parent looked back. Dae was thankful for she had collapsed into Amdreus' arms in sorrow.

Recuperation was proving impossible for Dae. The further the ship drew away from home the weaker Dae became. She spent most of her days aboard ship sleeping, fighting the growing washes of despair and discomfort that enveloped her. She began to see ghosts in places where no ghost ought to be, and when in company, other passengers appeared to be haunted by spirits. She felt as if she were slipping into madness.

She gazed blandly at her drawn face in the smoothened mirror in her tiny cabin. Her cheekbones were sunken, her lips thin and pale.

"Figson, is the grief making me ill? Making me mad?" she whispered to her silent companion. The shadow in the corner stirred but did not move. Her eyes watched it in the reflection of the mirror. The ship moved languidly with the surge. The captain had warned of rough seas and rain. She turned and watched the drops pelting the tiny porthole, the noon sky almost like night in the darkness of the clouds.

Unable to stand anymore, she reclined into her tiny bed and rolled herself up in her blankets. Staring at the wooden bulkhead, she closed her eyes and succumbed to sleep, shivering still underneath all the blankets, incapable of feeling warm.

Amdreus, unaware of Dae's failing health; but concerned by her pale and frail countenance, doted. The little slip of darkness was with Dae always. By the time the ship arrived at Mahalav's great port city of Velnam, Dae was barely able to speak. She was huddled into herself. She'd lost weight over the journey. Her colour was pallid and deathly, her eyes hollowed into darkened sockets. Her gown and redingote hung from her frame like a shapeless shroud. Amdreus bundled her into the coach he'd hired, and filled the seat bins with hot bricks. He let her huddle close to him, shivering; teeth chattering. She felt like a bundle of sticks against him. He was growing alarmed. Figson remained clinging close, sometimes wrapped around Dae like a shawl. Every so often, Dae's whole body would shudder with tremors. Amdreus, powerless and growing increasingly worried, held her close, willing the coach to move faster.

"Good gods, Dae!" Renna gasped and ran to her sister; behind her the phalanx of ghosts followed, all there to greet the absent family member. She was enrobed in spirits, but this time, it was a gentle welcome. Renna managed to find her way through the swarm and embraced her sister, looking at her with dismay. "You look terrible," Renna wept. "Just awful!"

"Bring her inside," Ammette called from the doorway. Amdreus and Renna helped her negotiate the stairs to the foyer, and Ammette gestured that they go straight up the stairs. Dae's legs buckled and Amdreus caught her, scooping her up into his arms.

He carried her up the stairs, with Renna at his heels, fussing over her sister with worry.

They could hear Ammette shouting orders for hot broth and tea, for a bed warmer to be filled with fresh hot coals, and for Dae's abigail to come at once. There was already a servant present stoking the fires in her bed chamber and sitting room when they swept in with Dae. The bed warmer sat in a coppery luster by the new flames, awaiting its contents. Amdreus grudgingly stepped away as the abigail and Renna took charge of Dae. Breathless, he leaned on the doorframe, watching. The many ghosts that had swarmed behind them up the stairs, and followed them into her rooms, hovered about. Renna shooed them away, but they circled still. His brow furrowed. The ghosts were unusually clingy and curious. Usually his presence made them disappear. He frowned, and on a whim, he shifted his sight to the shadethers, hoping to find a clue for their behavior. When the tint and viscosity of the air slipped into the murky depths of the shadether, and the living things faded into faded effigies, and the dead things came forward into bright focus. When the scene before him shifted, the hairs on the back of his neck bristled.

Renna glanced over at him, and frowned. "Mr. Drouwd, I appreciate your devotion, but you best leave now. We are about to undress her," she barked. He snapped back to reality and nodded gravely. Spinning on his heel, he swept out of the room in a flare of his greatcoat. Only a short moment later, the sound of hoofs battering away from the hall could be heard. Nobody paid any heed to his departure. Dae's needs were paramount, and she looked to be fading away quickly.

Amdreus flew off of his horse in a flurry, his boots hitting the snowy ground inside the small courtyard behind his house. He hurriedly unbuckled the girth and bridle and put his horse into its stall in spite of the steam rising from its sweaty coat. He drew the saddle and bridle off, and tossed them onto a roll of hay. "Roq, manage the horse please," he shouted. The words were meant for the boy that worked the stable, who had little to do for the past weeks he was away, and was napping in his small room above the stable. The shout was answered by a rapid footfall above. Amdreus didn't dwell. He left the horse in its stall and exited the small stable.

Hatter, having finally been roused from his blanket by the fire came barreling out to him the moment he approached the door and his wizened, crouched little housekeeper opened it for him.

"Mr. Drouwd, welcome home," she crooned. He nodded stiffly and circled her, shedding his hat and garrick and tossing them into her arms as she shuffled behind him. He walked to his private library and office, his favorite space; and barked for a fire before he shut the housekeeper out. Hatter followed, his whole body wagging in delight to see his master. But Amdreus was preoccupied. He looked around his office for a moment. It had late been tidied and dusted in his absence. A pile of letters from prospective clients was piled neatly on a corner of his desk. He took off his frock coat and threw it onto the chair, rolling up his shirtsleeves to his elbows. He then approached his cluttered bookshelf. He ran his finger down the row of spines. The afternoon was waning so he lit a candle to assist him in seeking out the book he wanted.

He was growing frustrated as he reached his last shelf and did not find what he had been seeking. He then knelt and opened the cabinets below the bookshelves, and began to sort through the riffle of papers and rolls, ledgers and other odds and ends crammed in there. In one of the cabinets where he kept his old, outdated ghosting instruments, he found what he was looking for. With a satisfied grunt, he gripped the edge of a wide, thick, fraying book from the bottom of a pile of instruments and papers, and pushed those back while drawing out the book from beneath them. A few things clattered onto the floor. He left the doors open and ignored the mess that had been disgorged onto the rug from the cabinet, dropping the large tome onto his desk with a loud bang. He grasped his candle and drew it near. He ignored the housemaid as she came in and quietly lit a fire.

He opened the cover and began to leaf through the yellowed pages. A work made with both parchment and vellum, the book contained a mix of text and beautifully rendered imagery painted by hand onto translucent pages. His leafing came to a sudden halt, and his eyes fell upon the image of a man depicted floating in the air, held aloft by a coterie of shades. His long hair was fanned out by the movement of the ghosts. But what was most notable in the image, was that the rendering depicted something Amdreus had witnessed when he viewed her through the shadethers; a tracing outline of red mist rising off the figure like the steam had done from his horse so shortly before. Hers was not yet as strongly depicted as what was shown in the image, but it was beginning to appear. He fell back against the back of his chair, which groaned from the force of the movement, and he reached up and put his hands over his face. "Good ghosts, Figson... what have you done?" he murmured from behind his hands. With a shake of the head, he got up and put his frock coat back on. He picked up the book, and stalked out, the dog ecstatically at his heels.

Ammette stared at Amdreus in incredulity, as if she wasn't quite grasping what he was telling her. Amdreus pointed to the image, looking at the older woman darkly. Hatter, sensing the strain, pined quietly by the fire. Not a ghost was to be seen, they were all with Dae. Their unusually strong attraction to her now made sense to Amdreus. He thought it was because Figson remained by her side even in places where the Shadethers were weak. It didn't seem excessive or strange until they reached Fallswell with its abundant hordes of ghosts when he realized it was a more than that. They were attracted to what she was becoming.
"The Eminence," he repeated. He pushed the open book towards her and she barely glanced at it.
"I know what that is," she grumbled. She stood and shuffled to the windows. "There hasn't been such a thing in this world for hundreds of years," She said distractedly. "How is that possible?"
"Figson did it. Figson died doing it." He turned the page, and looked at the intricate text. He put his finger down on the page. "Sacred to all, both spirit and man, Eminence rises from the power of deathwitches."
"What does that mean?" Ammette snapped irritably.
"The last Eminence to manifest in this world was here on Mahalav. It was made. Made by deathwitches. They sacrificed themselves to become one with it. I suspect Figson not only gave his powers and life force to Dae, I think he found a way to steal the power back from Eldus' heir, and give that to her first. It takes the

power of more than one deathwitch to draw magic from the shades, and to do what was done. I don't know the ritual; I don't know the spells or what he did. I don't even know where one could find that sort of information. But Figson had it, and Figson didn't just kill himself, he gave his power and that of his rival to Dae. He turned her into something this world hasn't seen in centuries. That's why the ghosts are flanking her. That's why the house is silent. She is an Eminence. She is transforming into it as we speak."

"Why?" Ammette blurted. "Why would he do that?"

"I can ask him, but I suspect he won't cooperate. But it's no mystery why he did it if you look at this text. It explains it quite succinctly. Figson wanted to give Dae the power to fix what can be fixed; to save her parents; for her and Renna to be free of risk. Eminences are the vessels of law for the death arts. Her existence, as it is now, means that her will supercedes any power the laws of the living may have assumed in the absence of the Eminences. No ghost or person can harm her. Not with what she is now," he said with an air of both lamentation and intrigue. "And no living man can exercise their own laws over what is her domain. Her mother and father's trial is now no longer valid. The living may no longer pass judgment on them. The Shadethers now have a representative in this world, and she must be obeyed."

Just as he finished speaking, the shriekers began to screech out all at once, the home began to vibrate to a deep resonating hum that felt as if it originated from everywhere. The shadethers were stirring in a way the Ghoster had never witnessed. He shouted, but his voice was obliterated by the din. Ammette gripped the back of a chair and looked upon Amdreus with concern.

Ghosts began to flit through from outside, coming in from other places; streaking through the walls, all heading in one direction; shriekers, howlers, shades and blots, terrors alike. The household stood in awe as the hum grew deafening.

Then in one fell swoop the din collectively silenced, and the house became deathly still.

There was the sound of approaching footfalls, and gasping. The door flew open and Renna was there, her face aglow.

"She's better. She's *so* much better!"

****

The four attorneys from Ghellick and Yaymes shared the long curving table that occupied the defense's side of the court. The five justices were just sinking into their towering chairs on the dais, their long, dusty-grey wigs hanging down onto their shoulders in long panels of powdered curls. They were the image of grim severity. The members of the prosecution also took their places. When everyone had settled down, the lead Justice hammered the gavel and the murmur of the court transitioned from whispers to silence.

"Bring the accused," he demanded. A door opened behind the gallery, and the Evlans appeared, both defiant and frightened. They were led to the box where they were forcibly sat into chairs. The bailiff stood behind them.

"Does the prosecution have anything to say before we deliver our judgment and sentencing?" Before the prosecution could say anything, a sweet, gentle voice rose up from the silence of the gallery.

"This court has no authority over these people," she said.

"Who dares speak out of turn? This is a grave offense!" one of the justices shouted, banging his gavel. The audience turned to peer in puzzlement at her, some faces familiar to Dae. They were her peers, watching the trial of her parents. She rose fluidly to her feet. Dae looked nothing like she had the short weeks before. Her frailty was replaced with an almost glowing presence, her skin flawless, her innocent freckles, her bright, striking eyes; all radiant. She moved with a confidence that was contrary to anyone who knew her nature. Gliding down the aisle towards the horseshoe where the attorneys were seated; the slip of a girl drew the attention of every soul in the room, including Amdreus' whose face was crossed with a warm, loving smile. The judges were even stunned by her appearance, so much so they did not order the bailiff to remove her.

"I beg you sit, young lady, or you will be forcibly removed from this court."

"Again, Your Honors, I reiterate, this court has no right to hear this case," she replied with a tone of authority. The audience murmured to one another. The gavel fell harshly and commanded silence. She stood directly before the judges, peering at them, her bright, guileless expression beaming up at their dour faces.

"I am sorry, Miss, if you cannot comply you will be removed," the eldest of the judges declared. Dae merely shook her head, and lifted her hand. There was a titter on the edges of the courtroom, up in the high seats, and then the murmurs spread inwards. Ladies squealed and people began to shift and stand. A small ghost flitted towards Dae, and then another. Then the horrifying shriek of larger, hideous apparitions came screeching into the room, and then the violent torrents of terrors, and black oily shadows of more ghosts, the formed bodies of the departed, the court room began to fill with ghosts. They swirled around Dae in such numbers, and with such power, that the gown whipped around her ankles.

The court's gavel banged on the wood as if it had sway over the intruding apparitions. Faster and faster the ghosts whirled around Dae, and more and more arrived, flitting through the stricken audience, and joining the growing maelstrom of the dead that swirled at Dae's legs. She began to rise from the force of their movement, the ghosts lifted her up, casting her upwards to be at eye level with the justices.

Amdreus could see the waves of power radiating from her body in bright blood red, rising up in steamy whorls. To the eyes of the ordinary people, she was sight to behold, her arms out, lifted on a great whirling cloud of spirits. The judges had fallen deathly still, and watched her.

"It has been four centuries since this world has seen an Eminence. They were deliberately culled from the world, in order to exercise control over the spiritual realm from this living world," Dae said sweetly. The people had fallen still, as did the shrieking ghosts. "But I am here now. And this trial is no longer yours to judge. These are matters of the shadethers, and this is my jurisdiction now. You may all go." Her pedestal of spirits began to lower, and she was soon placed gently upon her slippered feet again. The spirits then cast themselves outwards towards the audience, the ghosts assuming their most terrifying forms, sending most of the people screaming for the doors.

The judges and attorneys were petrified, but none of them exited. The Evlans were left to their own devices, and they chose to join Amdreus near the door—gaping incredulously at their daughter. Dae waited until the room was quiet enough to speak again.

"I declare Mr. and Mrs. Evlan innocent of all charges made against them," she muttered. "But the living world must have the true accused, mustn't it?" she said, looking with kindness upon the faces of Figson's former colleagues from Ghellick & Yaymes, then to the prosecuting attorneys representing the throne.

"So, I give him to you," she said. She reached into the pocket of her walking gown, and withdrew a small silver vial. She tossed it before her onto the floor between the opposing attorneys, where it skipped and rolled a few feet and then fell still. She stepped back. With a wave of her hand, the vial began to vibrate. A jiggling, quivering mass of goo disgorged from the open mouth of the vial, the colour of it was a mix of flesh and blood, and it writhed and boiled onto the marble tiles.

"What in the name of…?" one of the judges exclaimed in disgust.

"He won't be the same as he was before he was killed, I'm afraid, one cannot resurrect a deathwitch and hope for normality. They are too connected to the shadether to exist as revenants," Dae explained while the growing mass of flesh throbbed and expanded in spurts; bulges and appendages throwing themselves out from the lump, and slapping noisily onto the cool marble with bloody splatter. "I was left only with a little bit of his flesh to work with, but it was enough to give you what you have." The body was eating through the floor as it formed, drawing its mass from the ground itself; transforming the stone into the flesh and bone that was forming before everyone's eyes.

"I would normally preside over his case, but I will offer this court this last judgment on any case involving anything with the shadether. I trust you will make the right decision in regards to the crimes of this deathwitch. Your demonstration of good sense and rationality will be taken as a gesture of goodwill towards the shades. I will be assessing and eliminating the current laws as they stand, concerning the shadethers, and to repair what has been dismantled since the last of the living shades were lost to the living world. You may let this be known to all of the courts and the throne," Dae concluded.

The quivering blob of flesh had grown to about the size of a child, and was forming the rudimentary shape of a person, the hands and feet still indistinguishable. The head was still but a shapeless bulge, which at the moment Dae finished speaking, split open to reveal a gaping maw with partially formed teeth; strings of mucous and blood stretching grotesquely across the new opening. The carcass made an agonized raspy groan and writhed as it continued to accrete mass from the ground, and build new flesh upon its shivering body. Dae peered impassively upon it, and then glanced at the small ghost that remained close to her body. The only people that remained in the courtroom were a few straggling, intrepid observers, the attorneys and the judges. Amdreus stood in the gaping doorway to the hall, his arms crossed, a stern look upon his brow; her parents behind him, clutching hands, eyes wide and fearful.

The ghost of Figson resolved from his small, inconspicuous shape to a facsimile of his former self; the visible lines of his shape were strongest in the center around his head and torso, his arms and legs were indistinct and barely visible. His being was a soft misty grey with white highlights where the shafts of cold light from the grey day broke through the high windows and fell upon him. The attorneys of Ghellick & Yaymes gasped at the sight of their colleague.

"I am blessed to have the council of a modern attorney to help me with the tasks to come; the analysis of your laws concerning the death arts, and the modifications that will be required to meet the needs of the shadethers," Dae said. "You may inform your throne of these developments," she instructed them. "We expect the trial of this deathwitch to be expeditious and for his punishment to be appropriate and quick," she added pointedly. "From this point forward, the shadether will direct all crimes to me in its own way. The crown may no longer make arrests for death-crimes."

She then curtsied to each party, and turned, sailing with her ghostly companion to the door, where she joined Amdreus and her parents. They retreated, leaving the body of Eldus to continue its work to form a twisted, broken, tormented version of its past self, merely for the purpose of being sentenced to death. His screams from the wretched pain could be heard all the way out to the main entrance of the Garvash courthouse.

Epilogue

Mrs. Drouwd most inelegantly hurled the large stick into the air. It arced into the sky and then flew into the wheat field, where the swaying stalks were still new and bright green. Hatter bounced up from the deep wheat to gain his bearings, and bounded after the stick. Mr. Drouwd walked beside her, his hand wrapped around hers, his face an expression of amusement. She giggled as the dog popped up here and there, eventually appearing holding the stick. In the distance, the farmer was in the next field with his plough team, preparing for a winter crop. He shouted at them to get the dog out of his crop and shook his fist, which made her giggle even more.

Ahead, Renna and a Mr. Edger were walking as well. Renna was all timidity and blushes, covering her mouth whenever she laughed. He was a new face at Fallswell. There were much of those of late now that matters of the shades had become the responsibility of one person alone—so far. Ammette had embraced society in a limited fashion for the sake of Renna. She held a coming out ball for her, and invited all the finest people to visit.

Mr. Edger was the finest of all, as far as Renna was concerned. He came not through the society connections, but out of a scholarly curiosity about Dae. He, like many of the scholarly types, were intrigued by the appearance of the first Eminence to manifest itself in centuries; enthralled by the notion that the creatures of the shades were finally accountable to the shadethers, and not to the living world.

The lines between living and dead were at last balanced; the death magic bearers now subject to fair accountability, and not to rules based on fear by living beings. These were interesting developments for many. The bookish fellow arrived with a shabby hand-written card. Dae was immediately reminded of Figson in life, humble and slightly awkward; kind, but not forward. Renna liked him at once. She forgot the other suitors almost immediately. Renna's unexpected attentions also made him less obsessed with Dae and less determined to pelt her with continuous questions. How could she dislike such curiosity and earnest fascination? Especially when like Figson, there wasn't all that much more to recommend him to Renna. He spent almost every day at Fallswell. Dae and Amdreus were often called to chaperone the young couple. Even now as Dae's middle swelled with her first child; a sweet little lump underneath the high waist of her redingote.

Figson was a constant presence; a mostly silent one, but one that did not shy from making himself and his opinions known; especially when it came to Amdreus. Figson did not hide his jealousy of the man who now possessed the heart of the woman Figson loved. It was a constant nuisance, and a subject often raised when they occasionally bickered as couples do.

It was often when Figson deliberately spilled drinks or food on him at the table, or made books drop on his head when he was riffling through his cupboards. The ghost made him irritable, and he often threatened to obliterate him. But somehow, the strange household found a way to function and find contentment. Dae's pregnancy settled Figson down a bit, but he seemed to take pleasure in pestering Amdreus. And the first Eminence to return to the world for so many years, to whom he was married, existed quietly in his small cantilevered, wattle and daub house in the village of Sedge. The ghoster worked quietly to solve spectral problems, and the Eminence stitched her embroidery while simultaneously bridging the gap between the world of the living and the world of the dead.

GLOSSARY

abigail –a personal lady's maid.

aestrals –attendants who prepare a deceased body for burial.

Avasanne –A wild poisonous plant that if touched, can cause death or in rare cases prolonged coma.

channel –A participant in the burial ceremony who acts to channel and strengthen the connection of the spirit guide with the shadether so that the dead can make an safe transition into the world of the dead.

crosser – A casual or slang term for a revenant.

deathmark –A supernatural mark on the skin of a person who wields powers over the dead or the death world. Those directly affected by the powers may also carry such a mark.

death-skills –describing the possession of magical abilities related to the dead or the world of the dead.

Deathwitch –A person who possesses the power to resurrect the dead, to broach the veil between the dead and the living, and to cause possessions.

Echinn –A Westerly people residing on the isle of Echii who still openly practice death-arts.

Emzilla –A man who chooses to live as the nurturer, homemaker, who eschews a life of career and industry and focuses instead on the arts and child-rearing.

etherforce –Powers rooted in the world of the dead.

Etherman –A person who has the ability to see the presence of the shadethers, and to identify the strength and extent of a haunted site. They once served to facilitate the death-ceremonies, but now serve to contribute to the valuation of land and building sites.

ethersenses –The sense of those who possess death skills to detect and see into the world of the dead.

garrick –A long great-coat with a split tail for riding; some with many capes adorning the shoulders.

Garvash –A Southerly Island of the Island Nations of Heknos.

Ghoster –A person possessing the power to control and destroy ghosts and spirits.

Heela kestrels —Small, intelligent avian raptors with keen homing abilities. Used throughout the Island Nations for communication.

life-thief —A demon-specter, native to the shadethers, that hunts and steals the souls of the morally corrupt.

Magister — A representative of the royal court of law.

power-bearer —A general term for someone with magical abilities.

resurrectionist —A Deathwitch; someone who can resurrect the dead. A person who can draw spirits from the shadethers and construct new bodies for them to inhabit.

revenant —Someone whose spirit has been taken from the shadether and placed into a reconstructed body.

shadether —The shadether is the *veil* of the world of the dead. It is invisible to ordinary people. Although the shadether exists everywhere, in tandem with the living world, there are areas where the shadether is particularly dense and strong, (these pockets are opened by the practice of resurrections), allowing for the dead to co-exist with the living in the form of spirits and ghosts in the world of the living.

Shertrath —A rite of passage that is celebrated when the magical power of a predecessor is passed down to a younger heir. Sometimes it happens at birth, sometimes it happens later after the passing of an older, powered relative.

spectral tether —A bond which ties a spirit to the living world so that it cannot escape. It can only be applied by a ghoster.

spirit guide —A member of a typical burial ceremony, purported to assist the spirits of the recently dead cross to the shadether. Rather weak in the death-skills, they require the assistance of channels to complete their work.

Zillig —A woman who chooses to walk as a man; to eschew the life of a homemaker and to pursue a career, who wears the clothing styles of a man, and who is also the dominant person in the household.

About the Author

Miranda Mayer lives in the Mount Hood territory of Oregon. A polyglot, artist, avid historic costumer and lifelong equestrian; her interests are broad, and edge on geekery most of time. She is married with one child.

Miranda's stories range from Science Fiction to Urban Fantasy to Fantasy. She writes from her heart, imbues her writing with her quirky humour, and tries very hard to make her characters as real and three-dimensional as possible. Her unpredictable and rather Attention-Deficit-Disordered nature guarantees that her stories will take readers to unexpected places.

www.ingramcontent.com/pod-product-compliance
Lightning Source LLC
Chambersburg PA
CBHW021153130626
46554CB00005B/1796